With a jerk, Jacob twisted his head to the right and peered into the deep darkness, where seven decrepit zombies rippled and transformed into gray-skinned humanoids—dopplegangers! Jacob opened his mouth to shout, at the same time reaching for his sword. The closest doppleganger shoved its hand into his mouth, cutting off his air. The others tackled him, dragging him to the floor. Their hands reformed into spike-lined stocks that screwed themselves into the deck, attempting to pin the fighter down.

FORGOTTEN REALMS®
Fantasy Adventure

THE DOUBLE DIAMOND TRIANGLE SAGA™

THE DOUBLE DIAMOND TRIANGLE SAGA™

Part 2

THE PALADINS

James M. Ward and David Wise

THE PALADINS
©1998 TSR, Inc.
All Rights Reserved.

Distributed to the book trade in the United States by Random House, Inc. and in Canada by Random House of Canada Ltd. Distributed to the hobby, toy, and comic trade in the United States and Canada by regional distributors. Distributed worldwide by Wizards of the Coast, Inc. and regional distributors.

Cover art by Heather LeMay.

First Printing: January 1998
Printed in the United States of America.
Library of Congress Catalog Card Number: 96-90565

9 8 7 6 5 4 3 2 1

8635XXX1501

ISBN:0-7869-0865-3

U.S., CANADA, ASIA,
PACIFIC, & LATIN AMERICA
Wizards of the Coast, Inc.
P.O. Box 707
Renton, WA 98057-0707
+1-206-624-0933

EUROPEAN HEADQUARTERS
Wizards of the Coast, Belgium
P.B. 34
2300 Turnhout
Belgium
+32-14-44-30-44

Visit our website at **www.tsr.com**

Dedication

For Ceaser, whose healing powers surpassed a paladin.
David Wise

From my point of view, this work is dedicated to helpful
spirits, among whom I include my wife, Janean,
thanks for the sirloin steaks, smothered in mushrooms.
Life would be far more difficult without them.
James M. Ward

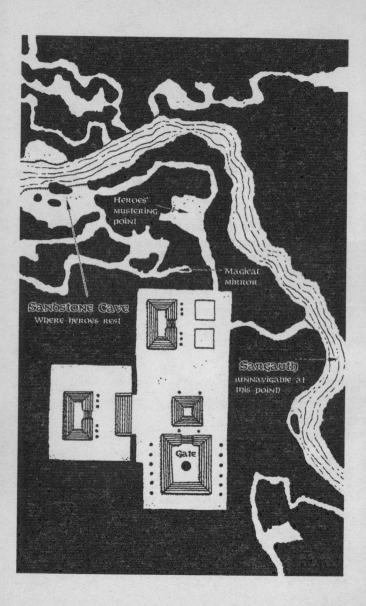

Heroes'
mustering
point

Magical
mirror

Sandstone Cave
Where heroes rest

Sangauth
(unnavigable at
this point)

Gate

Prologue

If a castle gate slams shut, Tyr is pointing to another castle, farther down.

Khelben "Blackstaff" Arunsun labored amid the tall wooden book stands and the long chest of tiny drawers, crammed with exotic components, in his spellcasting chamber at the top of his tower. He turned from tome to tome on the stands, reading and reciting, while green and red sparks buzzed unnoticed around his body. He shook his head disapprovingly at one manual, turning to a fat grimoire on the next stand and moving its dragon-skin pages with a wave of his finger. Magical energy crackled around his hands. Masterfully controlled rage lent power to his incantations. The bride of Piergeiron Paladinson had been seized in the middle of her own wedding, and because she'd been stolen under Blackstaff's nose, he was taking it *very* personally!

"The Utter East is tied into this somehow," he grumbled. "The bloodforges that created Lady Eidola's kidnappers came from there, but when I scry the Utter East, the crystal ball goes dark." As Khelben glared at the lightless seeing crystal resting on its onyx pedestal, an ancient spell designed to pierce magical fog, crafted by the great Drawmij of Oerth, popped into his head, and he snapped his fingers at the thought. He crossed his laboratory to a chest of scrolls and thumbed through them until he found the one he wanted, unrolled it, and absorbed the words.

"Savretun, soenlovenom," he muttered, memorizing intently. . . .

"Wake him up! He's sleeping and I can't wake him up!"

Sznapp! Red-fire sparks crackled and seared a huge human paw reaching out to touch the engrossed Blackstaff. Without shrinking from the pain of the wizard's personal shield, the massive hand shook Khelben roughly, breaking his concentration. He wheeled with a start and grimaced up at the eight-foot-tall Madieron Sunderstone. Piegeiron's personal bodyguard ignored the magical ward. The wizard made a mental note to increase the strength of his protection.

"What is it, Sunderstone?" he snapped.

"I can't wake my master! He told me to call Captain Rulathon, and when I brought him, my lord wouldn't wake up!" Madieron stammered, uttering more words than Blackstaff had ever heard him put together at one time. That meant real trouble.

With an arcane phrase, Khelben blinked to Piergeiron's chamber, where Captain Rulathon, second-in-command of the city, stood over his lord, slapping him once, twice, thrice, without eliciting so much as a flutter of Piegeiron's eyelids. As the red and green glow of the High Mage's appearance faded, the soldier turned with an expression of panic on his face.

"Wizard, he won't wake up!"

"If you're finished assaulting him, Rulathon, stand aside."

Blackstaff's eyes turned crimson, then orange, as he mustered his power. Guards rushed in as word spread of the new curse that had befallen Waterdeep's finest, only to spin and crash into others behind them while purple streaks of magic blotted out the chamber. Captain Rulathon stood behind Khelben with his arm thrown over his eyes, clinging to one of the bed's canopy posts to keep his balance in the bewildering light storm.

"You men," Rulathon yelled in the magical gale, "keep everyone out!"

"Perhaps it's some effect from the shadow warriors who stole Eidola," muttered Khelben's voice within the glare. "Perhaps it's something Eidola *herself* has done. . . ."

Rulathon started. "What did you say, wizard?"

The blinding light of the High Mage's art faded. He stood over Piegeiron's prostrate form, grinding his teeth. "I've tried everything possible here," he admitted angrily. "Lord Paladinson feared further treachery in the city, and he seems to have been right." Khelben furrowed his bushy black and gray brows. "Perhaps, on the matter of those paladins I should heed his advice, after all."

The High Mage turned to face Rulathon and ordered, "Summon the paladins of Phlan, Miltiades and Kern!"

"As you wish High Mage. When do—" A hissing *zap* cut off the captain's question. The bed chamber door swung open and a throng of sleeping guards spilled into the chamber with it.

"No one—*no one*—tells me not to come into my father's chambers!" snarled Aleena Paladinstar, striding in with a swirl of wizard's robes. "Father!" she cried, rushing to the bed. "Is he dying?"

"I don't know, Aleena. We need to find the people who took Eidola. Only they know how he was put to sleep, and apparently only they'll know how to wake him."

Khelben reached down and drew a chain from around Piergeiron's neck. Upon it hung a sphere of clear crystal. I suspect this will come in very handy now," he said, removing the gem and slipping it into his robe.

The elder mage looked grimly into the eyes of the younger. "I'm sending you and the paladins of Tyr to the Utter East, to find Eidola and her kidnappers. I wanted to send Force Grey, but your father was *adamant* they protect Waterdeep. He was equally convinced Kern and Miltiades should lead the rescue. This time, I think we'll respect his wishes. Meet the Phlan delegation in my tower. Let it be you who requests their help."

A grim look of determination cleared the worry from the lovely spellcaster's face. "Gods and fiends won't help whomever's behind this," she swore. "I'll talk to the paladins, gather a few things, then meet you all in your chambers." With one last, lingering look upon her sleeping father, she left the room. Judging from her expression, Khelben wouldn't give two coppers for the lives of the kidnappers.

"Rulathon, forget my earlier orders. Madieron Sunderstone is probably running here from my tower as fast as his oafish feet can carry him. Until he gets here, stand guard over your lord, and let no one else near him. I've no doubt Sunderstone will take it from there."

After making his own last check of Piegeiron, Khelben found his way out of the palace and slowly walked toward his tower, too spent to cast another teleport spell.

"Mage Arunsun!" called Laskar Nesher, waddling to intercept the High Mage. "Mage Arunsun, is it true Lord Paladinson has been struck down? Word is all over the streets! You must tell me what is going on!"

"I don't have to tell you anything, Nesher."

The portly merchant clutched at Khelben's arm. "But you know the trade pact with Kara-Tur depends upon Piegeiron, so the interests of the Guild rest with him as well!"

Khelben frowned down at Nesher's hand, then up at his face; Nesher let go. "Yes, I know. Tell me, guildsman, do you stand to make more money if the pact is ratified or not?"

Laskar started back. His chins waggled in distress. "*Surely* you must know the Merchant's Guild is *loyal* to the Nine Lords, and no member would *dream* of subverting the will of the Open Lord himself!"

"Get out of my way, Nesher, or every gold piece you touch turns to lead. . . ."

Laskar blinked at Khelben, considered how serious the mage might be, then hastily moved aside.

Chapter 1

Injustice anywhere is a threat to justice everywhere.

"Lords, you now know all Aleena and I know. I would appreciate your thoughts on the matter," said Khelben in his private council chamber, walled from its circular floor to its domed ceiling with overcrowded bookstacks. He sat at the apex of a large, triangular table of thick mahogany. The table's glossy surface swirled with curls of thick burgundy inlays flaring to crimson here and there and then dimming, as though fireflies crawled beneath the veneer. The inlays' enchantment rendered all languages into a tongue easily understood by those around the table. To Khelben's trained ears, lies spoken over the design resonated like tin.

To the High Mage's left and right sat Kern and Miltiades, while Aleena Paladinstar occupied an overstuffed chair at the base of the triangle, opposite Khelben.

The wizard settled back in his high-backed dragonhide chair and mentally activated its arcane ability. In extradimensional space, he saw peoples' auras glow and churn in patterns and colors. His eyes subtly shimmered as the magic took effect. Both paladins noted the reddish sparkle behind the wizard's pupils, but they said nothing. Just the same, Kern couldn't help but wonder if *maybe* glowing red eyes were an effrontery to Tyr.

Khelben's gleaming eyes first studied Miltiades and blinked against the blinding white essence of purity bathing the paladin, who sat ramrod straight in his chair. Even his graceful plate mail of ancient craft shone as brilliant as quicksilver in the sun. Here was a titanic force of order and law, with a presence of will capable of deflecting magic as a shield fends off blows. Although he appeared to be a man of about forty winters, Miltiades was 1,000 years old. Khelben's friend Elminster had once spoken of this knight, who died in the service of Tyr, was raised as a skeleton to quest for centuries, and was at last rewarded with mortality and love.

"You will need to send out a rescue party *immediately*. The enemy must not complete their plans," remarked Miltiades, a rolling burr in his speech. Unusually insightful if a bit cocky, this paladin had come to Khelben's conclusion without hesitation or pause. The tone of his voice carried the wisdom of many lifetimes and the brash confidence of affirmed heroism.

"Tyr loathes the injustice of personal attacks for political gain, and we shall be his tools on Faerûn," added the paladin.

"Praise be to Tyr," Kern intoned.

Blackstaff's eyes squinted as he scanned Kern. His bushy brow cocked. Kern had no aura! Where was the unmistakable glow of a paladin? Where was his life force, his lawful illumination, his shimmer of holy magic, his shining truthfulness? When Khelben faced other *null* individuals in the past, they usually turned out to be baatezu or tanar'ri fiends.

Khelben kept his surprise to himself. There could be several good reasons why the young paladin thwarted his detection magic: He might possess a magical item that gave proof against scrying devices, or he might be deflecting the magic. On the other hand, there were plenty of bad reasons, too. Kern, he observed suspiciously, was completely different from Miltiades. Where the elder wasted no motion and presented himself in few words, Kern was the opposite—always moving, even when seated. Oh, the youthful knight spoke like a paladin, yet not with the solemn depth of his comrade. He was too likable to be a paladin.

Like Miltiades, Kern carried his age well; he had passed at least thirty years but appeared to have lived only nineteen of them. Elminster had mentioned this one as well, saying he fought hordes of fiends to recover the famed Warhammer of Tyr and return it to its great altar in Phlan. Indeed, any who knew Kern's name knew no one could match him with a warhammer.

Paladins are such odd creatures, thought Khelben. Pledged to live by a strict code of virtue, they should be ideally suited to lead a rescue, yet that very same code made them impossible to count on. With their often-strange and intractable senses of honor, they frequently jeopardized themselves and their missions—and that lay heavily upon Khelben's mind.

"Miltiades has saved many maidens from myriad dangers," said Kern with a bow to his friend. "I am honored to take part in this rescue! I thank Tyr for the opportunity! The cause is just, the Open Lord is deserved of our services, and the crime of kidnapping is an affront to Tyr!"

"Tyr be praised," Miltiades echoed.

Aleena Paladinstar snorted in amusement. "The mere idea of saving a damsel in distress would make a paladin foam at the mouth." She rose from her chair, and Miltiades and Kern stood as well. "Oh, sit down, for Tyr's sake," she snapped, crossing to a nearby table laden with mugs and bottles and pouring herself a cup of wine.

"What is the fastest route to the Utter East?" she asked.

"A dimensional gate, of course."

"Is there such a gate in the Western Heartlands?"

"Yes," answered Khelben. "It's in Undermountain."

"Undermountain!" echoed Aleena with a grimace, crossing back to the mahogany triangle.

"Undermountain?" repeated Kern, curious.

Khelben continued. "I've searched my records on Halaster's complex and found a map that purports to be a fragment of the eastern side of the third level." He reached into his robe and produced a bright orange gem, which he placed on the table and spun, whispering a word of magic. The stone gained speed as it twirled and shot yellow light upward, forming a map out of the beams in the air.

"This is the place, here," he said, pointing at a chamber on the suspended image. "I'll give you the parchment map itself before you go. Find your way to this room and you'll find the gate. It's marked by a pair of mammoth tusks, rising out of a pyramid. This afternoon, after we assemble a team, I'll teleport the lot of you to an access point on the third level of Undermountain."

"Teleport?" asked Kern, coloring slightly. "Are you a *very* powerful wizard, Mage Arunsun?"

Khelben looked at the impudent young paladin with irritation.

"Why not send us directly to the gate chamber?" asked Miltiades. "Time is of the essence."

"Because Undermountain is the province of the mad mage Halaster, and to protect it he's spent years making it impossible to teleport in and out of the great subterranean complex with any accuracy. You'll have to sniff out the gate, yourselves."

Khelben reached out and snatched up the spinning gem, and the light map dissolved. "When you find the gate, you must activate it. Stand before it and say, 'Open in the name of the past and present Lords of Waterdeep.' Its other side lies, according to my texts, within a magic area where my crystal cannot see." Khelben's fingers tapped restlessly on the table. "I cannot see . . ." he muttered to himself.

"The gate will take us to a place the enemy has shielded from us?" asked Miltiades, thoughtfully. "An ambush, mayhap?"

Khelben lifted his head with a jerk. "Possibly. The gate in Undermountain is the only known portal to the Utter East. But that blind spot is the only place in the Utter East that could hide Lady Eidola from my magic. In any event, we have no choice but to begin with the gate." He rose and began to pace the chamber. "What if there is an ambush? Aren't you warriors? Aren't you prepared for a fight?"

"Of course!" cried Kern. "But how do we find the Lady once we've arrived in the Utter East?"

The wizard reached into his robe. This time he drew forth the crystal pendant he'd taken from the Open Lord. "I made this for Aleena's father. The closer you get to the Lady Eidola, the brighter it glows. Piegeiron wanted it to light his lady's way. I found the sentiment rather romantic, so I indulged him."

Aleena reached for it, then pulled back her hand. "Give it to Kern," she said. "He is renowned for having sought and found the legendary Hammer of Tyr, which was lost for years. He must be a great seeker, so he may be the best finder."

"Aleena!" protested Blackstaff, but she held up her hand to silence him. For a moment, she looked just like her father.

"The paladins must lead the team, Khelben," she reminded him. She pointed at the chain dangling from his hand. "With that, they can lead the way to Eidola."

Khelben frowned at Kern, who stood and gravely reached for the pendant. The wizard hesitated a moment more, then with a grunt of assent handed it to the paladin, who put it over his head and tucked it under his chain mail. "I'll keep it safe, Lady Paladinstar. You can count on me."

Khelben stood looking from Miltiades to Kern and back. "All Waterdeep depends upon you, and all the Lords thank you for consenting to undertake this quest. *I* must, however, insist upon three things, and I expect as paladins you'll honor your oath to abide by my demands." The paladins glanced at each other and then assumed positions of attention.

"One. You are to avoid all discussion of and involvement with the trade pact that the Lords of Waterdeep are negotiating with Kara-Tur. Your mission is to locate Lady Eidola, not to seek justice against those whose political motivations may well have prompted her kidnapping.

"Two. Your orders are to *locate* Lady Eidola and report her whereabouts, *not* reclaim her from the kidnappers. I do not—I repeat—do *not* want you to boldly go forth and fight for her freedom. If necessary, we have thousands of knights who can do that, but such an action on your part could get her killed! Should you be captured, the Lords of Waterdeep will *not* acknowledge your mission or your association with them.

"Three. Destroy the source of the magic inhibiting my scrying. If you're successful, I might be able to locate her, myself, and bring her back magically."

"Agreed!" blurted Kern. "That is, if Miltiades has no objections," he added. The elder paladin nodded.

"Aleena Paladinstar, a wizardess of the first rank and our lord's daughter, joins this rescue attempt," continued Khelben. "I expect you to defer to her authority."

Miltiades rose to stress his words. "I agree this mission must be conducted discreetly. Hence, Kern, the four other followers of Tyr who came with us from Phlan, and I are *all* who should go. I am against including Lady Paladinstar. With all due respect, the members of my delegation can get the job done more efficiently without outside help or interference."

Khelben stared at Miltiades. "Outside help? *Outside* help! This is a *Waterdeep* matter! There's much more at stake here than your *honor* as followers of Tyr!"

"Indeed, my honor may not be the only thing at stake, Mage Lord Arunsun, yet my honor is sufficient to assure the mission will be undertaken with as much success as anyone of Waterdeep," replied Miltiades evenly.

"I don't think you've quite *grasped* the situation. You've been requested to *aid* Waterdeep agents in the recovery of Lady Eidola."

"Kern and I are to lead the team. Was that not what Lord Paladinson decreed? Did not Lady Paladinstar say so just moments ago? As a leader of the quest, I choose the team."

Khelben leaned over the table, his eyes flashing with magical fire. "Look! You're going to be surrounded, not by monsters or thugs but by smiling liars who may or may not be the kidnappers! You *won't* find necromancers in black robes or stinking orcs standing against you! You probably won't even know the difference between someone who's trying to help you and someone who's leading you to your own death."

"If your simple three objectives are the whole of our quest, then Tyr will guide us surely and swiftly."

"*Simple* objectives!"

"Miltiades, Kern," interjected Aleena before Khelben exploded, "you are wise and courageous, both, yet will you deny me this quest? This matter involves my father and future stepmother. Waterdeep's interests *should* be represented, but my personal interests should be even more compelling."

Aleena looked deeply into Miltiades's eyes. "Please," she pleaded. "I love my father, and I can't simply stand by while his beloved is missing and he lies in a coma. For the sake of *justice*," she said, stressing the word, "let me offer my humble assistance in all things magical. I must do something to help or I'll go mad with worry. I am a talented spellcaster; I can help your group."

Miltiades gazed back at the beautiful spellcaster, and for a moment he spied a passion he often saw in the eyes of his own beloved Evaine. "All right, I wave my objection and you shall join the team."

Khelben quietly sighed in relief. At least one person he trusted would be there. "And you'll swear to strictly abide by my three conditions?" he prodded.

"Upon our honor as paladins of Tyr."

"Then good luck, all of you," concluded Khelben. "I just hope this isn't a mistake," he added under his breath.

"Let's gather the team!" cried Kern, beaming. "We're going to rescue a princess!"

"She's not a princess," said Aleena, glancing at Khelben with a slight grin and shaking her head.

Interlude 1

It's not whether you win or lose that counts, it's how much pain you inflict along the way.

Lightless fire shrouded the ground in a hypnotic, tumbling blur on the sixty-fifth level of the Abyss. It obscured jutting razors of flint, erect and barbed, like swarms of devil's-grass. Unwholesome blackness swallowed and choked the plane, and a constant echo of wind blew through the barren chasm, carrying upon it the distant wail of futile death. The reek of curdled blood hung like hot sewage in the bitter-cold air.

General Raachaak inhaled deeply and flexed his bony wings while the trace of a grin played across his toothy maw. The towering tanar'ri fiend crossed his muscular arms and tucked jagged claws under massive biceps, against his bare, crimson torso. A serpentine whip of manifold tails, studded with whetted shards of obsidian, coiled and hung from his belt of baatezu hide. Faintly glowing steam curled along his leathery red, oily skin, enveloping the pointed-eared balor in a miasma of evil.

Before him, three vulturelike vrock tanar'ri stood reluctantly, casting their avian gazes from side to side, as if they sought some escape. Their long, pointed talons sank into the hard stone, crushing flat the keen blades of Abyssal flint like crusty sand. A slime oozed from glands beneath their wings, spreading a film over their thick coats of black and gray feathers. Their wide collars of pinfeathers, shining with mucous, stabbed outward like filthy, curved needles. The skin of their scrawny necks and knobby heads folded and cracked like mildew-ridden leather, but their curved, pointed beaks were glossy and fierce. They hunched like scavengers devouring the dead, masking their thoughts from the telepathic greater fiend, concealing a desire to kill and consume him. The central vrock extended a hideous pair of shriveled humanoid arms from beneath his wings and wrung his craven hands together in a gesture of humility.

"You're to go to the Prime Material Plane," the general's bass voice boomed in their scaly heads, making them wince and flutter nervously. "To a feeble world called Toril by the miserable primes who live there— *humankind* and its ilk. There, in an ancient city newly resettled, the primes have unearthed a most delightful contrivance, one that conjures countless warriors out of thin air! When I acquire the dark of this device, this *bloodforge,* I'll raise an army large enough to overrun stinking Baator in a single roll of the Sisyphus Stone!"

The balor laughed aloud, filling the plane with terrifying glee as he spread his wings wide and unclasped his arms. The vrocks shrieked and capered in agony and delight. Abruptly, Raachaak stifled his merriment. His eyes widened, and he bared his pointed teeth, clenching his thick jaw while his amber eyes burned gold. His slimy lips curled into a sneer.

"*But* . . . there is a problem. The sniveling low-life berks who brought me this information first tried to take the prize for themselves, and they failed! Now, the primes have warded the city of the bloodforge against all tanar'ri. That's why I've summoned you."

General Raachaak glared at the servile creatures before him. "Shaakat, Rejik, Morbaat, obey or die as larvae in a swarm of ravenous chasme!" he bellowed into their sinister brains. "See the city and its place on that world as I picture it in my mind, and go! Discover a way into that city and return to me with the answer! A portal to Toril awaits on the third strand of Lolth's Web, on the next layer! Now go!"

"Shall *we* not capture this bloodforge . . . and bring it to you, General?" thought Morbaat, impulsively.

In a blur, Raachaak seized the vrock by the throat and lifted her over his head. "You dare turn stag on me?" he roared. He hurled Morbaat to the ground with crushing force, scattering Shaakat and Rejik, and drew forth his whip. With facile and wicked grace he unfurled the scourge, twirled it over his head with a long sweep of his burly arm, and brought its glistening, obsidian-laden strands down like tenebrous lightning. They rent the air and sliced through the lesser fiend's feathers, driving deep into her wretched body. Morbaat went rigid, convulsing in torment. She began to screech again and again, in an ever-rising pitch, dragging herself along the ground toward Raachaak's taloned feet as the whip rose and cracked. At last she crawled and screamed no more.

General Raachaak looked up for the other two vrocks, but they were already gone, probably through Lolth's Web and halfway to the Prime by now. The balor threw back his head and howled in potent self-exultation as he deftly coiled his leather and hung it at his hip.

Chapter 2

Fret not if you fall, yet lie in disgrace if you choose not to rise again.

"Before we all rode together to the wedding of Lord Piegeiron and Lady Eidola, we did not know well these other good followers of Tyr, who came with us from Phlan, m'lady," explained Miltiades as he introduced her to them.

"We know Able best," said Kern, presenting a warrior-cleric with iron-black hair, deep chocolate eyes, and a clean-shaven jaw that remained shadowed despite the daily razor. "He's revered in Phlan for both his puissant skill with the warhammer and his great clerical war magic."

The massive fighter in sturdy banded armor bowed gravely, eyes focused on the floor, and said nothing. But Aleena detected within him a great sadness, that of someone who has begun to question the precepts by which he has lived all his life, and who now feels himself adrift in a hostile world.

"If I am not mistaken, you have already made Jacob's acquaintance," continued Miltiades. "He has often quested in the Western Heartlands and, I understand, has occasionally gone monster hunting with Lord Paladinson."

"And Piegeiron slays dragons with the best of 'em!" said Jacob, capturing and kissing the wizard's slender hand with a wink and a grin. "It's good to see you again, Aleena, and it's *great* to serve Tyr, Piegeiron, and these two paladins of legend, all at the same time!"

Aleena grinned down at the charming, curly-haired blond. I see you're still carrying that two-handed sword," she observed.

"Aye," said Miltiades sourly. "And not a warhammer, though that is the true weapon of the followers of Tyr. I will say, though," he conceded, "Jacob has demonstrated nimble adroitness with the blade in a joust. Both Kern and I have challenged Jacob to spar. Not only has he acquitted himself well in swordsmanship, but he often quotes Tyr's proverbs between blows."

The paladin gestured and Trandon, a leather-clad fighter of some fifty winters stepped forward. His long silver-streaked hair was tied behind him, and he leaned upon a fat, ashen quarterstaff.

"I'm not bad with a staff, myself," Aleena told him as they shook hands.

"I would prefer to wield the warhammer as befits a warrior of Tyr," the man answered. "But I've seen many battles and haven't always emerged unscathed." Trandon held up his right arm. "A close encounter with a vampire permanently drained the vitality from this arm, normal as it might appear to you, and left me unable to lift and wield the weapon of my faith."

"I've a magical ointment that I think could heal you," volunteered Aleena.

"Nay, Lady Paladinstar," said Miltiades. "I have called upon Tyr himself to heal Trandon, but his arm remains too weak to swing a hammer. There is no cure."

Trandon nodded sadly. "Tyr's will be done."

"Trandon has spent many years wandering Cormyr, recruiting servants for Tyr," said Kern. "He is highly trusted by the Hammers of Tyr, a prestigious order of paladins."

"I'm not one of the Hammers," added Trandon hastily. "I'm not even a paladin, although I do follow Tyr's way. I was merely asked to represent the Hammers' good wishes to Lord and Lady Paladinson, as they are forever busy serving almighty Tyr."

"And this is Harloon," said Miltiades, introducing the last of the Phlaness group. "He is but nineteen years of age, yet he has already seen more than his share of dungeons and dragons."

"True enough, your Ladyship," said the tall, dark young man. "I've been a sellsword since I was nigh fourteen."

"Until you found Tyr?"

"You could say that, I guess. A few months ago, a complete stranger saved my life and lost hers in the bargain. I wanted to know who she was, but she died before I could ask her, and the only mark she carried was the scales of Tyr on her warhammer." Harloon looked at Kern and smiled. "I met Kern in Phlan, learned about Tyr, and decided I wanted to become a paladin."

"And I never met a more persistent student," said Kern drily. Much to the merciless amusement of his beloved elvish wife, Listle, Harloon followed the paladin around like a puppy dog.

"I'm pleased to meet all of you, and honored to travel with you," announced Aleena.

"Let us commune with Tyr as our quest begins," pronounced Miltiades. "Rescue is our cause, our cause is just, justice is good, goodness is Tyr; the rescue of Lady Eidola is the will of Tyr!"

"Praise Tyr!" the other men cried.

There was a knock at the door.

"Praise Tyr, gentlemen, but don't forget that Lady Eidola is beloved of my father, who is the benevolent law of Waterdeep," said Aleena as she walked to the door and opened it, revealing a teenager with sandy hair, cropped short. His clean, tailored vest and freshly pressed trousers contrasted oddly with a new pair of heavy leather boots he wore. His legs bowed slightly under the weight of a gigantic backpack, overstuffed and lumpy, clothing spilling from the top and sides. From head to toe he bulged with weapons: a broadsword strapped to his back under the backpack, a bow and quiver across his shoulder, a dart belt wrapped around his waist, a dagger tucked under the belt, a short sword sheathed at both sides, and a knife tucked in the back of his right boot, which promised to scrape his ankle raw if he hiked all day. His eyes twinkled with excitement.

"This is Freeman Kastonoph," announced Aleena, "known to his friends as Noph. He will accompany us in the rescue." The boy looked at the pretty spellcaster and blushed crimson.

All six men looked at each other and frowned. Miltiades raised his finger and opened his mouth to speak, but Aleena cut him off. "—*and* manage my supplies . . . as well as provide services to the group! Such as cooking and—and *polishing armor!*" Noph's expression of excitement turned to one of surprise and distaste. She put her hand on his arm to stop his impending exclamation. "You'll learn that my assistant has *many* talents, and I won't hear of dissent."

Miltiades closed his mouth and dropped his finger.

"I'm off to Khelben's tower for last-minute preparations. We leave an hour before sunset. Noph, why don't you help the paladins, and get to know them?"

Aleena turned and left the room before Miltiades could come up with a reason to leave Noph behind. The boy mutely watched her go, sighed hopefully, then turned to look sheepishly at the powerful warriors of Tyr. Kern, Harloon, and Jacob slowly approached and circled Noph, inspecting him with grave expressions. He clasped his hands against his chest and bore their examination passively.

"Er, how many of these do you actually *use* in battle?" asked Harloon, politely, pointing at Noph's weaponry. He glanced at his comrades and fought down a smile.

"Well—uh—I haven't actually *been* in a battle, sir, but I thought I'd try them all and see which one works best," replied Noph.

"*Interesting* approach. But are there any *non*lethal ways to tell when a weapon *isn't* working well?"

Kern and Jacob sniggered loudly; Miltiades silenced them with a glare. "Harloon," he said quietly. "You remember your first days of questing better than the rest of us, so we will leave it to you to be sure that Freeman Kastonoph is properly packed." The paladin turned and strode into his bedchamber, closing the door behind him. With a chuckle and a few winks, Kern followed.

Jacob bowed politely to Noph. "Farewell, Freeman Kastonoph. I go to pack my weapons. Mayhap if I should forget any, perhaps I could borrow some of yours." With a snort of laughter, he disappeared, leaving Harloon and Noph alone.

Harloon approached the young man and began stripping him of his weaponry.

"Hey, I'll need all this stuff if Undermountain is as bad as the guards say!" protested Noph.

"First of all," said Harloon, as he pulled the unevenly loaded backpack from the boy's back, "the danger is ten times worse than those sleepy Waterdeep guards could ever imagine. Second of all, Aleena may have designated you as the pack mule, but we both know better, don't we? Once we hit the trail, none of us can afford to carry *your* load, along with ours. Therefore, we're going to lighten it right now."

"I can carry it!"

"Not if your leg's broken."

"My leg's not broken."

"If you don't do what I ask, I'll break it." Harloon smiled pleasantly at Noph and opened the pack. He cast away three spare sets of clothing and an extra pair of shoes. Then he pulled aside a heavy blanket and looked underneath. "Have you *ever* cast a throwing star?" he asked, holding up a handful of them.

"Yes! . . . Once."

"Did you hit anything?"

"I—uh—I almost killed the cat."

"You were aiming at your cat?"

"Of course not!"

Harloon dropped the throwing stars next to the weapons he had already extracted. "Do you know how to use throwing axes?" he asked, drawing out two shiny new ones from the pack.

"No, but—" The axes hit the floor.

"Do you know how to use throwing daggers?"

"No, but wait. Those looked like fun and they looked eas—" Five shiny new ones rattled and rolled over the axes.

"Do you know how to use a pitching disk?"

"No, but those were real sharp and throwing them wasn't har . . ." Three freshly oiled ones tumbled over the pile.

"Hey!" cried Noph, grabbing Harloon's arm as the young man dipped into the pack once more. "Do you mind if I carry *something?*"

"Not at all. That knife in your boot is more than enough."

"But it keeps sticking me in the ankle."

Harloon gave an exasperated sigh, then burst into laughter. As he reached down to show Noph how to sheath the weapon in his boot, he started laughing harder. Soon, he could only kneel and wipe the tears from his eyes.

"Can I at least keep the throwing stars?" asked Noph and he too started to laugh.

"Quiet, Freeman Kastonoph, if you please!" called Miltiades from the other room.

They looked toward the closed door, then back at each other, and continued their stifled laughter. They engaged in mock tug-of-wars with every article of clothing in the pack, while Harloon explained the rudiments of packing light and life on the wilderness trail.

* * * * *

In his bedchamber, Miltiades gazed into a jeweled hand mirror, from which his beauteous wife Evaine looked back. His stern features melted and all his lines of concern smoothed away, making him appear almost as youthful as the boy. He was more than a thousand years old, but his soul-swelling love for his spellcasting wife made time a toy that he carelessly tossed aside whenever he saw her.

"I *know* it was to be but a diplomatic appearance at the wedding, my darling, but Piegeiron Paladinson *himself* has specifically chosen us for this quest! *The* Blackstaff Arunsun is handling the teleportation! With Tyr's blessing, we should return in a day or two. If you like, I shall ask Khelben to send us home magically. That way, we'll be home *sooner* than expected."

Evaine's image wrinkled its nose and looked sideways at him. "I don't suppose a rage of dragons could keep a paladin from rescuing a princess."

"This is most serious, my love."

"Of course, of course."

"I depend upon you to make Listle understand," he added. Kern's fiery-tempered mate would *not* enjoy this surprise any more than Evaine.

"Certainly. As usual, I get the hardest part. You just be sure to wear the pendant and ring I gave you for your birthday. And don't let any wizards cast spells on you—especially *female* wizards," she said, wryly.

Miltiades smiled. "I know you would like to come, and bring Listle along for that matter, but time is our enemy. Plans are made and we leave immediately." He sighed and gently touched the smooth surface of the mirror. "I love you, my Evaine. Tyr keep you safe."

"Tyr keep you safe, my only," returned Evaine as she faded from view.

* * * * *

As the party marched to Khelben's tower, Miltiades noted the transformation of Freeman Kastonoph. The young man's pack, shrunk to a third of its previous size, rode close to his back, cinched tight with good thick straps. A slim dagger rode at his hip and a larger knife rested in his boot. Two canteens hung from the sides of his pack. He might live more than a day after all.

The rest of the party stood ready in Khelben's laboratory a few minutes later, where Aleena joined them. She looked approvingly at Noph, who grinned proudly back.

"Please stand together on the granite platform," ordered Khelben. "There will be a few moments of disorientation, and you'll find yourselves in a rough cavern on the eastern border of Undermountain. Look for rooms that match the configuration of the map and thence find your way to the gate. Good luck, and remember your oath!"

"Khelben, I'm not sure if you can teleport me," stammered Kern.

"Of course I can!"

"Of course he can!" echoed Miltiades. "Just concentrate on lowering your resistance," he quietly added.

Khelben began his casting. His words contorted into impossible syllables, and sparks of green arose and began to circle the round, granite platform. The screen of brilliant embers grew higher, rising over their heads, until Khelben uttered a final word, which sounded like a blast of wind. The sparks flared with blinding intensity and went out.

The group stood in the middle of Blackstaff's room.

Kern coughed.

"What is this?" hissed Blackstaff, incredulously.

"Ah, sorry," said Kern, stepping down from the pedestal. "I was afraid this might happen. You see, my mother's a powerful sorceress in her own right, and that had an effect on me. Most times, magic spells don't work on me. My mother says I'm anti-magical."

"Anti-magical? *Anti-magical?* What in Waterdeep is *anti-magical?"*

"As I've said, spells don't work on me, although magical things still function around me . . . usually."

"That's why you have no aura!" cried Khelben, staring narrowly at the young paladin—*if* he was a paladin. Between the dopplegangers, the two-faced guildsmen, and the queer devices from the Utter East, which

spawned solid warriors out of thin air, nothing could be trusted.

"Well Kern, it seems your quest is at an end," said the mage.

"What?"

"If I can't teleport you down to Undermountain, then I'll have to send the others without you."

"That's ridiculous!" cried Able.

"Out of the question!" declared Miltiades. "Kern must go with us."

"If he can't be enspelled, there's no way I can get him to Undermountain."

"If Kern doesn't go, none of us goes," said Harloon.

"Fine! Then none of you goes. I'll send Force Grey, which is what I wanted to do in the first place! *I don't know you,* and I don't know how you'll deal with this situation—"

"Khelben!" called Aleena from outside the circle of warriors that closed upon Blackstaff. "Hold your temper."

"You defy the commands of your lord, Piegeiron," Trandon accused.

"*My* lord? Let's get one thing straight. Lord Paladin-son is not my *sovereign,* he's my *colleague.* Don't try to use him to push me around! You know, the more I think about it, the more foolish this whole plan sounds. . . ."

The warriors of Tyr erupted in protest. The word *honor* emerged from the din. Aleena tried to intervene again but could not make herself heard. Noph stood blinking. This is just like a meeting of father's fellow lumber merchants, he thought. They're all bickering for their shares. For a moment, he wondered if heroism was just an ordinary job. The thought made him angry.

"Hey! *Hey!* HEY!" he shouted, until the mighty wizards and warriors fell silent and stared indignantly at him. "Undermountain's right below our feet, isn't it? Why don't we just hoof it there?"

"Can we walk to the third level of Undermountain from here?" asked Miltiades.

"Well . . . we can sail there," answered Aleena, hesitating. "But you paladins won't like it." She looked toward Khelben, who threw up his hands and looked away, thoroughly disgusted. "We'll have to pass through Skullport."

"Skullport?" asked Jacob.

"A city of criminals, outlaws, and . . . undead," said Miltiades. His voice was filled with dread, as he recalled his own existence as a death knight. He sighed heavily. "So be it. Piegeiron wanted the paladins of Tyr to lead the rescue, and Kern is one of the two. Through Skullport it is."

Aleena's eyes met Noph's, and she smiled reassuringly, but her face fell as she turned away.

Interlude 2

Knowledge is power. If you destroy your teacher, it will be all yours.

A twelve-foot stone wall surrounded the city where the bloodforge was hidden, but a thousand barriers could not bar the way of tanar'ri, were they not magically enhanced with powerful wards—as *this* wall was. The magnitude of its impregnability surprised the vrocks. Shaakat and Rejik circled above the habitation, carefully avoiding the invisible border, for no magic or might would allow them to enter. To the humans below, the vrocks appeared to be common vultures circling some unfortunate, fallen beast outside the city walls.

"There," thought Shaakat to his confederate, pointing with his gaunt hand to a dome within an enclosed courtyard of a large building, near the south wall. "Smell it?"

"Yes! A dimensional portal. A *gate!* In that round-topped structure surrounded by human sentinels."

The fiends laughed at the idea of a mere human protecting *anything*.

"Who knows where the gate's other side may lie?" whined Rejik.

"The primes in that burg below, leatherhead. See those humans just emerging from the keep? Let's scrag 'em!"

The vrocks spiraled lazily downward, waiting for the pair of riders to clear the warded walls before swooping in. As they cleared the magical barrier, the humans seemed to sense their peril, for they kicked at their steeds and broke into a gallop, making for the forest beyond. Shaakat and Rejik clucked in anticipation of sport and pulled in their wings, dipping into a dive. They leveled off and soared just over the riders' heads, parting their black beaks and piercing the air with a terrible, deafening screech, which stunned both the horses and the humans.

With horrible screams of their own, the horses writhed in terror and tumbled to the ground, pitching their helpless riders over their heads. Shaakat and Rejik came about just as the horses regained their feet. The fiends slashed the poor beasts from shoulders to rumps as they streaked by again. Both animals wailed piteously and collapsed twitching. One of the humans, the one in metal armor, quickly rolled to her feet and drew a gleaming blade with a flourish, turning to face her adversaries. The other lay groaning upon the ground, dazed or injured by his fall.

Shaakat and Rejik alighted before the warrior.

"Go back to the Abyss!" she snarled and charged them.

"Come with us!" they jeered, spreading wide their wings to expose rows of glands along their sides. With a sickening heave, the vrocks flexed their sinewy bodies, and a sticky spray shot from the glands, covering the woman in stringy mucous. Her sword sliced at them, but the fiends disappeared, blinking two steps to her side.

The warrior spun to face them again and raised her sword . . . then cringed and buckled in sudden agony while spores in the mucous covering her sprouted and wormed their spiny tendrils under her skin, swiftly covering her with thick, sinuous vines. She opened her mouth to scream, and the vines quickly swarmed into her mouth, choking her cry. She crumpled to the ground and thrashed about with a gurgle, then mercifully fell still.

Shaakat and Rejik turned toward the man, who struggled to a sitting position, cradling one arm while he gaped in shock at the heinous murder before him. They hopped, birdlike, toward him, but he made no move to escape. His eyes widened, and his mouth fell open as they approached. He began to shake violently.

"There's a gate inside the building from which you've just come," said Shaakat's raspy voice in his head.

"Do not deny it!" squealed Rejik's mind.

"Where is its other side?" continued Shaakat, his arm emerging to clutch at the human's throat.

"Undermountain," thought the man in return, unwillingly. "Undermountain, far to the west."

"Undermountain," repeated the vrocks telepathically, "far to the west."

Rejik's pointed beak opened impossibly wide while Shaakat bent low. They spread their wings about the fallen human. And a single scream rent the morning air.

Chapter 3

We are exactly what we believe we are.

"Skullport lies beneath the southern sea caves of Mount Waterdeep," explained Aleena as the party floated in a large flatboat along the banks of the subterranean river Sargauth. "It's a highly magical, lawless community, crawling with shady dealers and cutthroat justice." Guiding the paladins through one of the most lawless cities in the world was going to be tricky. "Remember, you promised me you wouldn't cause trouble down here, no matter what you see."

Kern stood beside her at the bow of the vessel and nodded his head once more. "Lady Paladinstar, there'll be no trouble."

As she sighed, their boat passed under an archway and entered the grand cavern of Skullport. To their port side ships of every size rocked at anchor, thick tethers reaching below the flat, black water of the great underground bay. In the distance beyond the gently weaving masts, the travelers could see uncountable caves riddling the ocean-carved walls, right up to the ceiling, several hundred feet above. An immense tangle of rickety catwalks strung between them sparkled with thousands of dim yellow torches and lanterns. Glowing lichen crawled along the cavern walls, illuminating the vast open space overhead, and little orbs of bright light streaked through it.

"Look at the will o' wisps!" said Harloon. "There must be hundreds of them. Do they try to lead beings to their deaths?"

"That and more," Aleena warned.

"Look at those huge ones over there!" said Noph, pointing up at two gigantic spheres in the air. Great arcs of lightning shot back and forth between them.

"Those aren't will o' wisps," whispered Trandon. "Those are beholders!"

"*Beholders?*" cried the paladins, instinctively reaching for their hammers. Jacob instantly sprang to their side, sword drawn.

"Kern! Miltiades! *No!*" hissed Aleena. "We've *got* to keep a low profile or we'll be fighting the entire population from now until Doomsday!"

Reluctantly, the warriors squatted down and hid their weapons.

Fortunately, no one manned the decks of the vessels around them, except a bored crewman who absently paced the deck of a huge war galleon, staring up at the battling beholders. They slipped stealthily among the darkened crafts and continued on their way.

"So far, so good," whispered Aleena. "We're going to sail right past the city and go deeper into the cave complex by way of the Sargauth. Only a few dozen feet and we'll leave Skullport behind and be in Undermountain."

"What are these things floating in the water?" asked Noph, grabbing a boat hook and pulling one nearer.

"Noph, stop!" cried Aleena, a moment too late.

An elvish skull bobbed within reach, thanks to Noph's hook. As he recognized it, the boy recoiled with a yelp. Trandon ducked underneath the swinging boat hook with a disgruntled gasp as Noph stumbled back. The boat pitched sharply, precipitating a commotion of flailing arms and startled shouts among the rest of the passengers. Noph lost his balance and reeled backward, pivoting over the side of the boat as it rolled with his shifting weight. Harloon caught his lashing arm at the last moment and yanked it downward. Noph tumbled headlong into the bottom of the boat. A wave hissed through the party, as the vessel sloshed in the water and settled to rest again.

"Chaos child!" spat Miltiades. "Control him, wizard."

Noph gasped.

"Now what?" grumbled the elder paladin, turning to follow the boy's line of sight.

The elf skull had risen out of the bay and now hovered nearby on a cluster of white sparks. Able and the paladins instinctively lifted their holy symbols, but Aleena leaped forward and pressed down their arms.

"Don't do it! You have no idea what harm you could cause. Don't move an inch! Remember, we're trying to sail *past* this city."

The skull turned lazily in the air. More white sparks flared up within its eye sockets. It drifted to within inches of Noph's face and stared at him for a long moment; he froze, wide-eyed, gaping back at it. The bony visage lingered a bit longer, then moved on to Harloon and calmly inspected each member of the party.

At last, its scrutiny fell upon Kern. It wafted up and down his body, pausing to stare at his holy warhammer for a long time before drifting before his face.

The pale jaw began to move, and they all heard a whispering voice. "This is a safe haven to all traders and customers," the death's-head told them. "Keep thy unwelcome weapons and thy uncivil tongues sheathed lest ye suffer my misery for all eternity."

Kern reacted without thinking. He reached out, placed his palm over the slimy dome of the skull, and invoked his divine healing powers. "Rest ancient one," he intoned solemnly. The skull sighed with pleasure, crumbled to dust, and fluttered into the dark waters below.

"Kern, no!" cried Aleena. Before the echo of her alarm bounced off the cavern walls, the water around them began to bubble frenetically. Hundreds of skulls boiled to the surface and surrounded the boat, just out of arm's reach. Their eyeless sockets trained upon the heroes, stared balefully, and their whispering voices spoke in unison.

" 'Tis forbidden to interfere with the watchers in the waters," came the chilling tones. "Now thou shalt perform a service or pay with thy lives. Each must lend aid to a zombie of Skullport before leaving."

"Not likely!" Harloon retorted. Able blanched.

"Oh yes you will!" said Aleena as she moved to the tiller and steered their vessel for the docks. "You don't understand the nature of this port. If the skulls make a demand, you *must* obey or shadow monsters *make* you obey."

"We can deal with such creatures," scoffed Kern.

"But even if you beat them, more appear, and they keep on coming. Sooner or later, they'll get to you. And we're in hurry, remember?"

The warriors snorted derisively, all but Trandon. Aleena looked angrily at Miltiades. "Look, this part of Faerûn is *my* turf. I know the rules, and you promised to follow them! This is what we're going to do: We'll dock and spread out. As long as you don't make trouble, no one will bother you, and *no one's* going to make trouble, right?"

The men nodded grudgingly. Harloon looked at Noph and said, "You stick with me." Noph grinned and nodded eagerly.

"And be *very* careful, Noph!"

The boy beamed and answered, "You, too, fair lady!" His voice cracked slightly. Jacob and Trandon exchanged grins.

"This won't be tough as long as you don't make it so," continued Aleena. "There are hundreds of zombies performing menial tasks in this city. Find one and help it. If the thing is carrying something, take it and follow the zombie to its destination—whatever you need to do to be of service. Got it?"

Miltiades grimaced at the city and nodded curtly. "It will be done." The entire group nodded reluctantly. Able looked toward the docks with profound sadness in his eyes. "So many lost souls," he murmured to himself.

"We will help as many zombies as we can, eh Able?" the plated paladin said with a grim smile.

"Just help *one* and get back here as soon as possible, *without* causing any trouble!" snapped Aleena. "If you're not back in an hour, we'll assume that you couldn't restrain yourself and give you up for dead, and we'll move on."

The boat hit the dock, and Noph and Harloon tied it up while the others entered the deadly depths of Skullport. As they dispersed, a group of shadowy figures trailed after them.

* * * * *

Kern could have kicked himself as he stalked the dockside streets. It wasn't the requirement to serve a zombie that galled him so much as his promise not to cause any trouble. As he paced the alleys, he was amazed at the evil and horror, everywhere he looked. Pale-skinned vampires walked the streets and ordered skeletons about while octopus-headed mind flayers consorted casually with black-robed wizards! Of course, no paladin could singlehandedly destroy *all* of the evil, but it would have been glorious to try. For better or worse, he concluded grouchily, there was simply no time for it.

"There's my zombie in need," he muttered, noting a group of four long-dead sailors who dragged large gray bags along the boardwalk. A juju zombie led them, waving a dark wand. The young paladin slipped ahead of the shuffling undead and hid in a blind alley. When the juju rounded the corner, the paladin slapped the wand from its desiccated hand.

"Aaaa, what hav yu done?" groaned the master zombie. The four zombies quickened their pace and stumbled into the alley, followed closely by the juju zombie. In the relative privacy of that dark cove, Kern lifted his hand in blessing. "I shall help you," he whispered. "In Tyr's name you will all become dust, and be freed from your undead suffering."

* * * * *

In all Miltiades's years of existence, both as a man and a death knight, he'd never seen anything as depraved as Skullport! Undead shambled everywhere, making his skin crawl with disgust. Ghosts walked side by side with necromancers, fighters lustily offered their swords to any who would pay gold, no matter what the job, and ordinary humans walked quickly, with heads bowed and fear in their eyes. The ancient paladin followed a main street into the heart of the cave city, keeping to the plentiful shadows. In an open square, he discovered slaves for sale on massive blocks, beholders arranging to hire mercenary bands, and even a pair of baatezu fiends gathered in a dark tryst.

He closed his eyes and prayed to Tyr for guidance, and in answer, his oath to Aleena rang in his ears. Shaking his head regretfully, he spotted a large sign that read "Zombys 4 sal." Miltiades passed through the door beside the sign and looked about in revulsion. There were dozens of undead, including women and children, dead dwarves, dead elves, and many, many dead sailors, all in various stages of decay. They stood immobile against the walls of the large room, panelled over with rotting planks of knotty pine. The ones closest to him began to slowly crumble into dust in the glow of his holy shield but they made no move. Each held a tag in hand, listing its price in gold pieces.

"Whoa! You're a little lost, aren't you?" remarked a skeletal warrior, approaching from behind a rack filled with dark wands and coming to an abrupt halt ten feet from the holy warrior. "Would you mind stepping outside? You're dissolving the merchandise!"

"I am here to help," offered Miltiades.

"I said *leave!*" snarled the undead fighter, jerkily unsheathing a rusted sword and cocking his arm to slash at the knight. Miltiades parried the blow easily with his shield and unhooked his hammer from his belt in the same motion. As the skeleton drew back to swing again, the mallet swept upward and connected with the bony jaw, sending it spinning through the air to shatter against the wall. The monster staggered back a step and caught itself, but Miltiades followed closely and pressed his holy symbol into its chest plate, crying, "In

Tyr's holy name, rest ancient warrior!"

A pile of dust plopped to the floor and puffed up in a cloud where the skeleton stood. Miltiades walked about the perimeter of the warehouse, disintegrating zombie after zombie, helping in the only way he knew how, by sending them to their final rest. A few minutes later, he exited with tears in his eyes. He'd accomplished Tyr's work that day.

* * * * *

"Undead everywhere! By Tyr, how can this be?"

Able shivered and pressed himself against a tavern wall on the streets of Skullport. Sweat beaded on his brow and dripped into his bulging eyes, burning them at the corners. His breath caught in short heaves and gasps. He gaped fearfully from side to side.

Shame welled in his heart, for facing undead was the last thing he wanted. The last time he had attempted to put the fear of his god into the walking dead, they had nearly killed him, ignoring his holy symbol in favor of his throat. Now, as he stood in the shadows and trembled, it wasn't the fear of death that terrified him, it was the fear that he no longer even possessed the power to repel evil.

"Am I lost to Tyr, or is He lost to me?" he wondered.

Zombies and skeletons wobbled by in droves. Overhead, several levels of catwalks rattled with the stilted footfall of dozens more. Across the way, a vampire hissed and berated a skeletal warrior for its insolence.

"All-powerful Tyr, how could you even allow a place like this to exist?" lamented the cleric.

The vampire noticed Able and peered suspiciously at him. The cleric immediately stood erect, positioning himself for a confrontation without yet drawing weapon or holy symbol. He stared back at the creature defiantly, but a hot prickle of fear crawled up his back. The vampire bared its fangs, eyes burning. Then it uttered something under its breath to the skeletal warrior, and both undead turned and walked around a corner. Able inhaled deeply and let it go, closing his eyes in relief. He stood there for a few moments, quelling his stomach.

A slight scrape on the ground to his right jolted Able to life. With a start, he leaped away from the sound and raised his hammer and shield.

A zombie watched him apathetically. He had wandered into its path. As Able looked upon the decaying thing, it occurred to him that the creature had once been a boy about Noph's age. Whatever life that had once surged through the body had been forever ripped away, leaving only a husk to stagger on until it finally crumbled to dust. It wasn't fair, wasn't *just*.

"Filthy monsters!" he growled. He lifted his warhammer and brandished the holy symbol emblazoned on it, crying, "Behold the light of Tyr and *rest!*"

The zombie continue to stare, disinterested.

Able bowed his head. A tear found its way down his bristling cheek. "Forgive me my weakness," he begged and shifted his grip on the hammer to destroy the zombie with two powerful blows. If he couldn't put it to rest with the power of his faith, at least he could do it with the power of his good right arm. He tossed the body into the river and snuck back to the ship.

* * * * *

Laskar Nesher, Noph's father, had warned his son about Skullport, mostly to scare him into minding when he was a child, but Noph had never believed the stories—until now. "It stands to reason," he thought bitterly, "that my father would know about a place like this." As he and Harloon made their way along the docks, they passed a long bank of caged monsters. Many thrust their talons toward the humans, yet their screams were inaudible, blocked by some evil wizard's spell to silence their pain and fury. Most of them possessed the bulbous eyes or pale coloring of Underdark dwellers.

"These are probably on their way to the surface, to be harvested for spell components," said Harloon with distaste. "We should destroy them all right here, so nobody suffers!"

"That won't help a zombie, Harl," said Noph. "The skull in the water said to help a zombie, and Aleena told us to keep out of trouble!"

"All right, all right! Let's check out that tavern over there."

The two young men crossed the boardwalk to a sagging, flat-topped building lit by a magical torch on each side of its thick, iron-shod door. Harloon grasped a fat metal ring, bolted to the door and pulled on it, releasing a puff of smoke and the heavy beat of dwarven music from within. As they peeked inside, they gulped at the sight of orcs, giants, and men carousing together, drinking from great ceramic flagons, and ogling scantily clad dancing slaves. Zombie waiters cleaned tables and brought drinks.

"Let's go find another zombie," said Harloon, shocked by the lurid atmosphere.

"No, this is perfect!" answered Noph, grabbing Harloon's breastplate without taking his eyes from the festivities. "We'll clean a few tables for the zombie servers and be gone in, say, five minutes—maybe ten."

"Noph, you're supposed to be following my lead."

"Look, Harl. Clearing a few tables doesn't get much safer. This time, *you* follow *me.*"

"Well . . . okay. Let's just get this done with, shall we?"

They entered the tavern and blended with the crowd. The music pounded in a deafening beat, so Noph simply pointed at the nearest zombie, obliviously clearing a table. Harloon nodded. They each snatched a dirty rag out of the apron off of passing zombie and started wiping down the tables around them.

"Hey now, I never asked to have my table washed," a huge goblin complained, glaring up at Noph.

"Management's policy, great noble. And today you win a drink on the house. Enjoy!" Noph dropped a silver piece on the table, and the goblin showed a toothy grin. That would buy it several ales.

A dancer leaped from the bar to a table that Harloon was clearing and leered down at him as she swayed seductively. He stumbled away, modestly dropping his eyes, and backed into a table flanked by duergar, knocking over their ales. They leaped to their feet to avoid being soaked by the beer and then closed around the young fighter with furious snarls on their lips. Duergar at nearby tables spotted the commotion and rose to join their kin, surrounding Harloon. Their poisonous pikes gleamed in the candle light as they drew near to the human's face. Other creatures noted the rising tension and backed off, looking forward to the show. Seven duergar against one human—the fight wouldn't last long.

Suddenly, a fat purse hit the floor next to the duergar, spilling its coins amidst their feet.

"Hey, that's my money!" cried Noph in a high-pitched voice and the room erupted into chaos as the surrounding drinkers dove for the gold. Harloon shoved two of them aside in the tumult and wormed his way free of the pile of bodies.

"Thanks! Let's get out of here!" shouted Harloon.

"Wait!" answered Noph. "Grab that zombie before it walks into the middle of the fight!" he cried, doing the same for another mindless creature.

"That takes care of our service to the zombie!" said Harloon. "Now *let's get out of here!*"

Noph flipped a silver piece to a dancer as they left. "Thanks for everything!" he called over his shoulder. Outside, they bent over and rested their hands on their knees while catching their breaths. They looked at one another and Harloon shook his head, an exasperated grin on his face. Noph returned the smile, with an added chuckle. Each reached out and clasped the other's shoulder.

"Let's get back to the boat," said Harloon with a cock of his head toward the water.

"I'm with you. Let's go."

* * * * *

Trandon had been terrified of the skulls that floated around the boat. His senses, more finely tuned to the rhythms of magic than the rest of the men, could see the deadly power. He also saw the shadow monsters floating above the water, around their boat, but he dared not say anything.

"Stupid youngling," he griped, blaming Noph for the delay.

The long-haired warrior quickly walked the narrow streets of the city until he was sure none of the others were anywhere near him. The undead of the city didn't bother him at all; necromantic magic was simple stuff. On the other hand, the magical powers openly displayed in the city disconcerted him gravely. Fiends sprouted out of arcane circles drawn on the very streets! Even more strangely, no one seemed to care! The fiends appeared without alarm and flew away into the darkness while others flapped down from above and spiraled into the complex patterns on the ground, slipping off to their native planes. Meanwhile, a human wizard marched pompously down the middle of a wide avenue, flanked by a fire elemental on each side.

"Idiot," Trandon muttered to himself. "The slightest slip and those monsters'll break free of their bond, and he'll be the first thing they kill."

Down a side street, he found a zombie limping along on the stump of its ankle, carrying its own foot. Trandon reached into a pouch that lay between his chest and his leather breastplate and drew forth a prickly pair of burrs. He let the zombie walk past him, then caught its broken limb and whispered a few words while pressing the burrs against the ragged end of the leg. Quickly he snatched the foot away from the creature and pressed it against the stump, uttering a last syllable. With a flash of reddish light, the foot adhered to the leg. Trandon released the zombie and watched it walk away, only slightly more graceful.

Trandon carefully looked from side to side, spying for onlookers—most especially other members of his party. It would be supremely difficult to resist using magic during this mission, but no one must know he was a wizard. He must maintain his cover at all costs.

Satisfied that no one had seen him, he stood up and made his way back to the boat.

* * * * *

Jacob skulked along the pier. It would be easy to find a zombie loading or unloading a ship somewhere nearby. He was in a hurry to finish the unpleasant business and get back to the boat, yet he couldn't help but exalt in the thrill of the adventure. There was nothing more exciting than questing for the glory of Tyr.

Several ships down, Jacob found what he had been looking for. Three wide gangplanks stretched from the dock to a barge, and a crew of zombies, alone and in pairs, offloaded wooden crates of various size. The lowly undead moved mechanically up and down from the cargo hold, hauling heavy boxes across the planks to deposit them on the dock. Apparently their handlers had set them to work and then wandered into a dive tavern across the way, for nothing sentient monitored their progress.

Jacob charged up the gangplank and crossed the deck, checking to each side for live crewmen. He bounded down the hole in the ship's main deck, into the cargo hold, and paused while his eyes adjusted to the darkness. No one had left a lantern, as the zombies needed no light. After a few moments, he made out a pair of walking dead close by, lifting a crate together. Jacob pushed one of them aside, tripping it over his foot. It tumbled to the ground and he stamped on its neck, crushing the bones with his boot. The zombie shuddered under his weight and fell still.

"Here, allow me to help," he whispered in a cracked voice.

Along with the other monster, the man lifted the crate. He squinted through the darkness, across the crate's upper side, at the decayed face of his co-worker, which stared back at him without recognition. Pity filled his heart, and Jacob thought that if he were a paladin, he could put this poor creature and all of its fellows to rest. Perhaps, when this quest was completed, he would receive an invitation from the *Knights of Holy Judgment,* or better yet, the *Knights of the Holy Sword!* That latter group of Tyr's paladins wielded blades, just like him. He and the zombie began to move together, toward the steps, but the undead sailor came to a stop at the base, and wouldn't begin its climb.

"Come on!" urged Jacob. "It's time for me to go!"

At that moment, he realized he was not alone among the dead.

With a jerk, he twisted his head to the right and peered into the deep darkness, where seven decrepit zombies rippled and transformed into gray-skinned humanoids—dopplegangers! Jacob opened his mouth to shout, at the same time releasing his side of the box so he could reach for his sword. The closest doppleganger shoved its hand into his mouth, cutting off his air. The others tackled him, dragging him to the floor. Their hands reformed into spike-lined stocks that screwed themselves into the deck, attempting to pin the fighter down. The first assailant's hand liquified in Jacob's mouth and oozed down his throat. He seized that one and began to tug at its arm, gagging against the intrusion. If he could only roll on top of them, he might be able to reach his sword. . . .

* * * * *

"I ran into a bit of trouble," Jacob admitted when he joined the party, back at the boat. "But no one noticed and I handled it quickly."

"How did you help *your* zombie?" Kern lightly asked Aleena as they cast off and headed back into the bay.

"I opened a door for one."

"That's good enough?"

"That was good enough for me."

"These creatures understand law," observed Miltiades, "but they know nothing of its spirit."

They rowed to the mouth of the cave that led upstream along the Sargauth, and as the grand cavern of Skullport curved down to meet them, the skulls once against boiled up from the deep. "Hast thou performed thy service as commanded?" they whispered. "We shall know if thou lie'st."

"Oh, we helped them, all right," answered Kern.

Aleena seized his arm and squeezed hard, silencing him. "We have done as thou ordered, Watchers," she declared solemnly.

Silence closed over them. The gentle lapping of water against the boat filled the air. "Then pass," whispered the voices, and the skull sank into the depths once more.

The paladins dug in deep with paddles and began to force their way against the Sargauth's deep, slow current. Behind, the dim light of Skullport faded completely, as Aleena pulled a magically lit beacon from her pack and placed it at the bow.

"Don't they even want to know what we did for their precious zombies?" asked Kern, looking back.

"No!" snapped the wizardess, "and neither do I!"

Somewhere deep in the void beyond, a crazed voice erupted into fits of laughter. The hilarity escalated to hysterics and then faded away.

"Who was that, Aleena?" asked Noph, unnerved.

"Halaster, the mad mage. This is his territory." She sighed dejectedly. "I *really* hate Undermountain."

Interlude 3

Don't worry about your debts if you've got friends, because a friend in need deserves what he gets!

"This is it!" thought Shaakat to his fiendish accomplice. "This is the gate! The scent of its magic is the same as the gate in the city of the *bloodforge*."

The vrocks stood at the base of a short, pyramid-shaped platform, upon which two massive ivory tusks of some prime creature sprouted and curved together, forming an arch. The uprights were deeply grooved along their lengths and inlaid with some magical metal shimmering and changing color like liquid chaos.

"Thank hideous Juiblex!" spat Rejik as he squatted down to rest upon the lowest of the glossy, crimson stone steps leading up to the gate. "This cage is a horrible death trap! I don't think we even scratched the surface of this—this *Undermountain,* but we've already killed a slithermorph, six ibrandlin, those two illithids with the nasty staves, a score of undead, three groups of heavily armed primes, and a sodding *herd* of beholders, not to mention those ill-tempered reflections of *us,* that came out of that mirror back there!"

"Yes, we must develop a place like this on the Abyss," agreed Shaakat.

"Let's go home and tell General Raachaak we've found the way into the city of the bloodforge!"

"Or—perhaps we should take the bloodforge for our own," returned Shaakat.

Rejik's beady eyes narrowed. "You would suffer Morbaat's fate, addle-cove?"

"Raachaak isn't here, stinkfeathers. Besides, if we capture the bloodforge, we can destroy him and ascend."

"*We?*" sneered Rejik.

"We . . . for now," growled Shaakat.

Rejik squinted up at the gate and clicked his beak pensively. "If we fail, we'll be turned into lowly larvae and left for the chasme on the Plane of Infinite Portals."

"We are true tanar'ri!" howled Shaakat. "Or *I* am, at least! You disgust me, baatezu's bastard!"

Rejik stood up and thrust his narrow face toward the other fiend. "I'm tired from all the killing, today, but I still have the energy to throttle you, berk. But go! Go through the gate and see if you can find the bloodforge before I return to General Raachaak and make my report. We'll see who ascends and who wriggles under a chasme's stinger."

"Fool! We have more power than we can imagine at our wingtips, and you want to run home to whine to a balor! So be it! Let us see who'll be a molting lackey, and who will command the bloodforge. I'm *not* afraid!"

"Have fun on the other side, fighting those sentinels," sneered Rejik. "Remember how tough the primes we encountered down here were? Ha!"

Shaakat paused, recalling the wounds he had suffered in this curious subterranean labyrinth, at the hands of humans, elves, and dwarves in armor. Once or twice, he admitted reluctantly, they had had to flee the battle, although they came *that close* to winning those fights.

"Exactly," chimed in Rejik, reading his thoughts. "Do you think we can simply step through this gate and take our prize? We may well not be enough. Remember what Raachaak said? Others have failed before us."

Shaakat gazed up at the portal, then craned his scrawny neck around to look over his feathery black shoulder, at the vast complex behind them. "I have an idea," he thought. "It will require the both of us to succeed, but it *cannot* fail. Rejik, will you ascend, and never fear Raachaak again, upon a bold stroke? Will you join with me . . . for now?"

Rejik stared at the other vrock, pondering. He hissed ruefully, "First, tell me your plan."

Chapter 4

A young warrior in the best equipment ever made is still a young warrior.

"Noph, you aren't planning to use that boat hook, are you?" Jacob asked sharply. Noph had been watching a pair of glowing eyes under the water beside the boat for several heartbeats. He'd thought of trying to hook whatever the eyes were—at least it was a distraction from all that spooky laughter in the darkness—but

Jacob's tone dissuaded him.

"Of course not," he answered. "I was just securing the hook. Has anyone else looked over the side of the boat lately?"

"Yes, but don't worry about it. We're at the end of the line."

Ahead, the cave ceiling narrowed, ending their boat ride. Aleena moved the tiller to angle toward a cave mouth to the side, which led up and out of sight. Harloon hopped into the water and dragged the boat to the shore. Noph gasped and leaned over the side, watching for the eyes in the river.

"Sdop dhere," a voice boomed.

"Doll, you musd pay a doll," another voice shouted.

"Dheir lighds so brighd," bawled another.

"Shud up, 'ficial doll keepers can'd be bodhered by lighds," scolded a fourth voice.

The party quickly drew their weapons and leaped to the shore. Three immense creatures with two heads apiece stepped out of the cave shaft—ettins! Each of the monsters carried a stone club the size of a man in each hand. They wrapped themselves sloppily in dark brown cave bear hides, covered in a thick layer of crusty dirt. Their wild, wiry hair grew long and unkempt, and their large teeth thrust at odd angles from their puffy red mouths. With their large, watery eyes and upturned, piggish snouts, they resembled freakish orcs.

"We no fighd widh you if you pay doll," the right head of the middle ettin claimed. "We keep dhis area clear of monsders. We ged dolls for dhis."

"We led everyone pass who pays doll," said the other head, resting its two clubs on the ground. "You have sheep or caddle?"

"Aleena could blast these brutes," suggested Noph, casting a worshipful look at the enchantress. "That would send them running."

"Wait," interrupted Miltiades, pushing Noph back with his warhammer. "These *very* intelligent creatures are attempting to provide a service. I suggest we deal honestly with them and be on our way."

The ettins smiled at the compliment, displaying their rotting teeth.

"Dhad's righd," said the first one. "We very indel . . . imbled . . . inbred . . ."

"Smard," supplied its other head.

"Righd. Smard."

"If they perform a useful service, they have every right to expect a fee," said Kern.

"Looks like dhey don'd have caddle," remarked the left head of the ettin on the right.

"Or sheep," added the other head.

"Could we make dhem bring sheep back?" asked the left head of the last one.

"Nod likely," answered the right side, sadly.

"Now what?" asked Aleena.

"Look," interrupted Noph, "I know all about ettins; there are lots of stories about them in Waterdeep. They're big, but they're *stupid*. We give 'em a little light show and they'll back right down."

"Sdupid!" cried the ettins.

"If dhey god no sheep, dhen dhey looks like lunch do me," the leader's left head snarled.

The middle ettin reached behind its back and produced a coil of clean, silky rope. Its gigantic hand clamped upon one end of the hemp while it flung the rest toward the heroes. The loops unfurled gracefully as the rope sailed through the air, and a circle opened perfectly to settle over Kern and Miltiades. With a distressing crunch, the rope yanked them together. The paladins fell to the ground, and coil upon coil of the rope lengthened and wrapped around them.

The three ettins brandished their clubs and roared

as they closed in to fight the rest of the party. Aleena pointed her finger and uttered a sharp command, and streaks of light shot from her fingertips, striking the giants. She directed three of the shafts at the leader, which howled in pain and tumbled to the ground, letting go of the rope; neither of the other ettins took notice of the jolt to their bodies. They screamed in anger and came on harder.

Able and Harloon moved to intercept them with their warhammers while Jacob drew his sword and Trandon brought his staff to bear, moving in upon the shins and knees of the ettins. Noph grabbed for his boot knife while stumbling back from the giants' charge. He tripped and rolled into the river with a loud splash, only to emerge a moment later, glancing over his shoulder for the glowing eyes.

Aleena waved her hands, and a hypnotic swirl of lights danced in the air. The giants' dull eyes followed the lights even as they pressed the attack. One swung at Harloon, only to feel Able's crushing blow at the back of its knee. The wounded ettin bawled in rage and spun around, opening its back to the swordsman, who landed another biting attack. The second ettin struggled against Jacob and Trandon. That left the third one, the leader, which climbed unsteadily to its feet, still smoking from Aleena's first attack. Noph waited for the tower of muscle and sinew to stand fully erect, then charged with his knife, aiming for the heel.

"Noph, duck!" screamed Harloon, breaking off his attack. He pushed the young man out of the way, as the ettin made a vicious swipe with its club. There was a sickening crack and Harloon's body fell twitching to the ground. Noph hit the dirt and rolled between the feet of the ettin. He carved a gash in the monster's ankle, came to his feet, and spun about with a smile on his face, until he saw Harloon lying close by.

"Harl!" he screamed, heedless of the monster standing over him, its club raised to smash in his head. The ettin bellowed in triumph as it waved both clubs aloft, but five brilliant missiles drilled into its chest, boring a hole straight through. It stood there for another moment, looking down at the gap in its body, then collapsed on top of Noph. He grunted under the weight and struggled to push the horrible-smelling body off of him.

"Free us from this Tyr-blasted rope!" ordered Miltiades, who still lay on the ground, bound with Kern. Jacob and Aleena rushed to unwrap them while Able and Trandon stood behind. With a few tugs on the loose end, the coils relaxed and tangled normally about their legs. The leaders rose to their feet but fell silent at the sound of sobbing behind them. Slowly, they turned to behold Noph, cradling Harloon's bloodied head and shoulders in his lap.

Somewhere in the caves beyond, distant laughter mocked the fallen hero.

"What have I done?" Noph wept, rocking his silent friend, back and forth. The warrior's eyes stared lifelessly. "He saved me. I would have died if he hadn't pushed me down." Tears streamed down his face. "Does he have parents? Someone will have to tell them. I should go back now . . . to tell them, I mean. No one should die in the darkness like this. Can I take him up and bury him in the sun? We can't just leave him here. What are we going to do? What am I going . . ."

"Noph, you're babbling," said Trandon. "Get up!"

Miltiades knelt down next to Noph and shut Harloon's lids. "He died well, Freeman Kastonoph, but we must move on."

Noph looked up at the paladin, shocked. "And just leave him here?"

"Indeed. The quest must continue."

The boy began to sob through his words. "Harl worshiped you, as well as Tyr! He gave his—his *life* for me and—and you expect me to walk away from him—leave him here? Is that some kind of—of *honor?*"

Miltiades stood erect and looked down severely upon Noph. "Foolish youngling, we have *all* lost friends—friends whom we have known for years. If Harloon died saving you, honor him by finishing what he started."

"But we can't just *leave* him here!" protested Noph. "We *can't!*"

"There will be time to mourn him when the quest is completed," said Kern. "Come on, Noph. Be strong."

"I don't *want* to be strong! My friend is dead!"

"I have an idea," Aleena intervened. She knelt next to Noph and stroked his hair. "I have an idea, Noph. Let's put him in the boat, set it on fire, and send it down the river. He would have liked that."

Noph looked into her eyes with a mixture of adoration and tears but did not speak.

"Freeman Kastonoph, he saved your life," said Miltiades. "If you honor Harloon, then justify his death by completing his quest."

Kern and Aleena helped Noph up. "After we finish rescuing Lady Eidola, I'll introduce you to Harloon's parents," the red-haired paladin offered. "They're merchant folk. You'll like them."

Able delivered a prayer for Harloon's quick passage to the Seven Heavens while the paladins chanted. Trandon and Jacob poured oil over the boat. Aleena drew a candle from her pack, anchored it in the floor of the boat, surrounded by the black oil, and carefully lit it. They launched the craft with Harloon resting at the stern, one hand on the tiller, the other on his warhammer. Aleena cast a spell as it drifted away, and the tiny flame of the candle flared brightly, touching off the oil. With a *whoosh,* flames swept over the vessel and its noble occupant.

Noph stood silently gazing at the flames. How could the paladins claim to be men of goodness and light, and abandon their fallen? he wondered. They didn't deserve Harloon, who would never let *them* down!

When the light of the bier had disappeared around the bend, Noph looked down at his feet and spied the coil of rope, barely noticing that it had magically wound itself up.

"Can I have this—to keep in memory of Harloon?"

Aleena waved her hand over the rope. "I detect no harmful energies," she said. "If no one minds, I think it'd be fine for you to keep it." The rest nodded assent.

Jacob and Trandon moved to the point position as the party prepared to move into the caves of Undermountain with only a fragment of map to show the way. Miltiades walked next to Noph.

"Freeman Kastonoph, you fought passably well in your first combat. I salute your courage. However, we are likely to be tested again before we complete our quest, and more may die. We will *not* have time to treat others as we did Harloon. Grieving is appropriate, but we must mourn *after* the quest is completed."

"Yes, sir." Pretentious bastard!

"Let's get moving," said Kern. "The princess awaits."

"She's *not* a princess!" insisted Aleena.

In the darkness ahead, the laughter burst forth again.

Interlude 4

When you lose control of the situation, just keep lashing out until you feel important again.

"Rejik, keep those manes under control!"

"I can't help it. The reflections keep trying to attack each other."

The vrocks stood between two massive groups of lesser fiends, all jostling roughly amongst themselves; inarticulate obscenities echoed through the corridors around them. Hundreds of manes—bloated little creatures with pointed ears and noses, and spindly stalks of wiry hair growing from the backs of their heads—spread out of sight, filling the corridors of Undermountain with a horrendous din. Tiny slugs and leeches crawled under their colorless, fatty folds of skin as they jabbered incoherently and scratched at each other. Their pale, bulbous eyes seeped with yellowish, poisonous pus, which they wiped on their gnarled claws while they quibbled. To the other side stood dozens of brutish bar-lgura, looking like gigantic orangutans with savage lower fangs, surveying the army around them and shaking their heads balefully. They seemed to shimmer and blend with the stone walls beside them, as though they would disappear if they remained still.

Shaakat and Rejik cackled at their own ingenuity. The power required to beckon and command so many denizens of their cruel, chaotic native plane would have required weeks of exhausting work, but in Undermountain thanks to the power of a magical mirror they had found, they only needed to perform a summoning once for each type, lowly mane and sturdy bar-lgura. The floor-length glass lay embedded within the stone wall of a rough cavern, not far from the gate to the Utter East. Unadorned by any frame and unremarkable until the vrocks wandered within its radius of reflection, the device conjured perfect copies of the fiendish beings summoned by the vrocks. Now, instead of expending energy to muster troops, they labored magically to keep them from attacking everything in sight, especially each other.

"If the bloodforge can create obedient soldiers like the mirror creates berserk fiends, *nothing* can stop us," thought Rejik.

"*Now* you think like a true tanar'ri," returned Shaakat. "*Now* General Raachaak'll have to deal with *us!* Come! Let us lead these miserable troops to glory and power."

The vrocks flexed their telepathic powers. The manes squealed in protest, like a host of butchered pigs, but they turned and crowded after the vulturelike master tanar'ri, pushing and shoving. The bar-lgura frowned at the irresistible orders and grouchily complied, blending in with the screaming horde. In a river of shrill chaos, the fiends rushed toward the gate to the Utter East. They flowed into the terminal cavern and pooled around the two evil leaders, who ascended the platform and stood before the gleaming aperture. For a moment, the masses fell silent, instinctively bracing for a surprise attack.

"Victory!" cried the vrocks together as they strode through the archway . . . and to the other side of the platform, without teleporting anywhere.

"Passworded!" snarled Shaakat in sudden fury. "The gate is passworded!"

His rage swept over the troops, who promptly dissolved into anarchy. They turned and charged out of the chamber, surging into the corridors of Undermountain, shrieking madly as they fled. A party of wandering drow, who had been approaching stealthily to investigate the disturbance, suddenly found itself overrun by the rampaging manes. The dark elves desperately tried to escape, then to defend themselves from the murderous throng, but died screaming. And the stampede continued.

Chapter 5

When things go wrong, try not to go with them.

"We've been going east for hours, now," groaned Noph. "We've got to be close!"

The party stripped off their backpacks and sat in a cavern with just enough floor and head space to accommodate the seven of them. Its smooth limestone surfaces, streaked with strands of burgundy and brown blended like pools of color, spilling and swirling together. The rock gracefully bent and turned at right angles, creating natural seats for the weary heroes. Irregular rifts in the walls and ceiling led in every direction, but three large passageways branched off from the chamber—one to the southwest, from which they'd come, one to the southeast, and the third due east. A distant cacophony rumbled in from the passage to the east, perhaps a crowd of creatures or the rush of the sea.

"Still no sign of any room that appears on this map of Khelben's," said Miltiades, studying the parchment under the light of an enchanted jewel. "This mazework of caves and corridors required the work of a twisted genius!"

A whisper of laughter echoed through the hallways.

"You're welcome," scoffed Jacob to the darkness.

"Actually, we've been extremely lucky," said Aleena. "We've only encountered a handful of monsters, and most of them were of the bite-and-run variety."

"That's because somebody else has already been through this area," replied Miltiades. "We've certainly encountered a lot of bodies."

"Who do you suppose wiped out those beholders back there?" asked Able. "Whoever did it, I hope they're on our side."

"Many groups of adventurers wander these hall-ways, honing their survival skills," said the wizardess.

"I'd say whoever killed those beholders is ready for dragons," said Noph.

Trandon stood and walked a few steps into the eastern corridor. "Whatever's making that noise, it's getting louder."

Kern got up and joined him, staring into the impenetrable darkness ahead. He concentrated on the noise, trying to decide if it was a mass of voices or blowing wind. Without warning a wave of nausea drenched him. He staggered back from it, his vision spinning. Trandon lunged for him as he fell. The warrior caught the young paladin in his burly arms and lowered him gently to the floor.

"Tyr save us!" sputtered Kern. "I've never felt so much concentrated evil in my life!"

Miltiades stepped into the shaft, steeling his nerves against the assault that overpowered Kern. Bitterness stung his heart like wet hornets, and he turned away from it. While the others looked on, he marched over to the northeastern corridor.

"Evil in that direction as well, but not so strong as from the east."

"Time for justice!" swore Kern, struggling back to his feet and glaring down the east shaft. Jacob drew his sword and stood next to him. Trandon tucked his quarterstaff into the crook of his arm and took up a position behind the swordsman.

"But what of the evil in the other direction?" asked Aleena.

"There's evil *everywhere* down here," said Miltiades. "Besides, I don't want to separate the party. It's too dangerous."

"Then let's send a small group, just to spy it out," suggested Able. "We don't want to be caught from behind."

"They're right," said Kern. "I'll go investigate it alone."

"No, I'll go," volunteered Able. "If that much evil radiates from the east, you two should stay here in case whatever's down there comes this way. I'll just peek in this direction and be right back."

"Trandon, you're light on your feet," said Miltiades. "Go with him."

"Right." Trandon swung around to the northeastern cave mouth.

"If it's okay, I'd like to go, too," said Noph. The paladins looked at him doubtfully. "I mean, I'm not even wearing armor, so I can sneak better than any of you. I promise I'll be careful."

"All right, but don't start anything," cautioned Kern. "Just check it out and get right back. And hurry. We've got a princess to rescue."

"I'm telling you, Kern, she's not a *princess*," growled Aleena.

The trio crept down the water-carved passageway and slipped around the bend. Soon, the backward cast of their dim blue light faded from view of the cavern where the rest of the party waited. The passage stretched on for several hundred feet, cutting a crooked path that turned toward the north. A few cave links large enough for one person to squeeze through branched off here and there, but they kept to the main shaft.

The party reached a sharp turn and paused. Around the corner, they spied reddish light.

"Can you see what it is?" whispered Able. The others shook their heads.

"I'll crawl up there and see if I can get a better look," hissed the boy.

"Be careful, Noph. Be very, *very* careful!"

Kastonoph drew his dagger and clenched it between his teeth. It forced him to pull his tongue way back into his throat and felt uncomfortable, but it did give him a fleeting sense of confidence. He dropped to his belly and wriggled around the corner, making his way toward the source of the light. Quietly he shimmied into a shallow depression of the cave floor. He clawed his way to its opposite rim and peeked over, looking into the cave beyond.

A hulking, brutish creature, with reddish-brown fur covering most of its body and gray flaps of skin along the sides of its face stood with its knuckles resting on the floor, looking into a mirror. It grinned wickedly into the glass, baring its long fangs, and lifted one forehand to flex its six digits in a grotesque wave at itself. Noph choked back a gasp.

The mirror began to glow brilliantly, and the beast

covered its eyes with a hairy paw. A low hum swelled, followed by the shrill snap of lightning sparks. Before the boy's amazed eyes, a red-furred, six-toed foot stepped from the mirror's smooth surface. A second later a duplicate monster fully emerged, paused a moment while it checked its footing, and then drew itself up before the other. The new arrival snarled and raised its hackles at its twin, and they began to slowly circle one another.

Noph took advantage of the moment to slip back toward Able and Trandon.

Something against the wall next to him shifted. . . .

Noph caught the movement out of the corner of his eye and froze. He tensed his muscles for a spring and dug his fingernails into the soft sandstone, then raised his buttocks as he shifted to his knees, finding purchase for his toes. His eyes and nostrils flared wide. With a final deep breath, he leaped up and forward, grunting with the effort. His hands left the ground as he shifted his weight to his feet and pushed off for all he was worth. A cool breeze slid through his hair as he accelerated.

In a flash, a massive claw shot out from the cave wall and snatched the boy by the collar. His feet swung out in front of him with a jerk as his forward momentum came to a sudden stop. Another one of the creatures, somehow camouflaged against the cave until now, lifted him by the back of his shirt and grinned cruelly into his eyes. Noph gawked back at the thing and opened his mouth to scream, but no sound came out.

"Stop!" shouted Able, who stood two paces away. The creature looked his way with a start. "Filthy Abyssal bar-lgura! You shall not have him!"

Trandon came to the cleric's side and twirled his quarterstaff threateningly. "You shall know and fear the power of Tyr!" he cried, pointing at Able. "This priest carries the god of justice within him!"

At Trandon's words, Able started and froze. He held forth his warhammer with Tyr's scales of justice emblazoned on its head, but no words came to him. Trandon looked at him with a frown of concern, and both the bar-lgura and Noph paused in dread, watching him—yet nothing happened. Five more bar-lgura stepped away from the walls. They were joined by the two from the room beyond.

"We feel nothing!" sneered voices in Able's head. "No power of Tyr. All we sense from you is . . . *fear.*"

"Able, call upon Tyr!" urged Trandon, taking a step back.

"Feel the power of the Abyss!" whispered the telepathic voices. The bar-lgura released their aura of terror and Noph screamed. Able and Trandon fell to the floor as though they'd been run over by a war wagon, crying out in horror themselves. "Tyr-slime, unloved by Tyr," the bar-lgura sneered. "We shall eat you alive and take this man-boy back to the Abyss, where he will be turned into a larva!" Macabre laughter rang through their heads.

"No!" shrieked Able. "Tyr, why have you forsaken me?" He looked at the wretched tanar'ri leering at the boy, who dangled helpless before them. Suddenly, his fear turned into fury, and he climbed to his feet. The bar-lgura looked at him, surprised.

"No, I say!" declared the warrior-cleric. "You shall *not* have him! If there is justice in this or any world, *I* shall have it, *wherever* I stand!" He looked at the fiends before him with a wild glint in his eyes. "Your evil power is nothing before justice! *Nothing!*"

The symbol on Able's warhammer caught the dim light of the chamber and flared to brilliance. A wave of screeches passed through the fiends. The one holding Noph dropped him to the ground. The symbol burned brighter still, bathing the entire cavern in holy white light.

"My *god!*" uttered Trandon, somewhere beside him, amazed at the sudden burst of power. "Noph, come to me! Come to me! Come now!"

Pure energy such as he had never felt filled Able, surging through his body and flowing into his hammer. He dropped to one knee and held his blazing holy symbol high. "Justice!" His voice resonated through the cavern. "Justice *is* Tyr, and He is Justice. So long as it lies within me, so does my god!"

With an ear-piercing howl, the nearest bar-lgura exploded! The one beside it threw back its head and shrieked in agony, then shattered into ichorous shreds while the rest began to wail and stumble toward Able, claws raised.

"Noph, *run!*" cried Trandon. The boy turned at the sound of his name and blinked uncomprehendingly at the cleric, then burst to life. He scrambled in the sticky mess splattering down from above, dropping his dagger. The screaming bar-lgura began to move with him, pressing toward his friends, so Noph grabbed at a furry leg and used it to catapult himself by, sliding toward his comrades and tripping the fiend in the process. It went down with a thud and ruptured, spraying flesh everywhere. Trandon leaped forward and seized the boy. Together they rolled away from the carnage and made their way behind Able.

"Run!" ordered Able. "Run for the others!"

"We won't leave without you!" Noph yelled.

"Go! For the quest!" He turned back to look at Noph for an instant, his eyes beaming with surety and light. "For justice!"

A bar-lgura seized Able by the neck and lifted him in the air. "Run!" he screamed. Then the fiend swept its massive claw with a snarl, ripping his head from his shoulders. Trandon and Noph bolted down the corridor, the slap of heavy paws on the stone at their heels.

As Trandon ran, he seized a ring upon his left forefinger and turned it; a blue glow rose on its surface.

"What are you doing?" panted Noph. At that moment, a hairy hand caught his ankle and tripped him. Trandon ground to a sudden halt, spun about, and threw out his pointing finger in the face of the two remaining fiends. A streak of jagged, radiant blue lightning shot forth, catching them both in its electrical fork with a peal of thunder. They bellowed in pain, fell over Noph, and disappeared!

"Noph?" cried Trandon. "Noph!" He dropped to his knees and searched the ground with his hands, refusing to believe his eyes. "Noph!"

At the sound of approaching footsteps, he looked up. The rest of the party stormed into the corridor and skidded to a halt.

"What's happened?" demanded Miltiades. "Where are Able and Freeman Kastonoph?"

"Dead," said Trandon.

"What happened?"

"We came upon fiends—tanar'ri, bar-lgura in a room with some sort of magical mirror in it. They caught Noph, but Able—"

Trandon's eyes brimmed and spilled over. "Able called upon Tyr, and it was *glorious!* I've never seen such power! He saved us, but they got him, and then they got Noph. I killed the last ones, but it was too late, too late!" He bowed his head and wept. "I've never seen anything like it!" he insisted through his sobs.

Kern and Miltiades looked at one another; the latter smiled with brimming eyes. "May Able be sitting by Tyr's side even as we speak," he intoned. "I knew he'd make it."

Somewhere in the distant complex, a fearsome cry went up. The screams of a hundred evil things filled the corridors, followed by the sound of a stampede.

"Whatever it is, it's coming this way!" shouted Jacob.

"Tyr's blessings on us all!" declared Miltiades.

Interlude 5

No one succeeds without a little bit of good fortune, and the luckier you are, the smarter your stupid plans look.

Kastonoph lay on his side before the gate to the Utter East. His wrists were bound to his ankles behind him, and his body was racked with agony from arching backward so sharply. So much for his service to Khelben and Piegeiron. So much for his heroism. Shaakat and Rejik had trussed him up and tossed him upon the platform and were laboring to reestablish control over the remaining manes and bar-lgura around them. When the wailing of the troops finally subsided, the vrocks turned their attention to their human captive, helpless and useless.

"How is this gate activated?" boomed Shaakat's voice within Noph's head.

"Get out of my mind, fiend! I won't tell you!" snarled the young man.

"Then you do know," said Rejik, aloud. "Open your mind, human. Open it to us. . . ."

A wave of bitter magic washed over Noph, scrambling his mind, obliterating thoughts of his predicament. Through the nauseating jumble in his mind, it occurred to him that he should cooperate with the fiends and tell them what they wanted to know.

"Bid the gate to open in the name of the past and present Lords of Waterdeep," he told them. "That will activate it."

"Well done, slave," thought Shaakat to the magically charmed prisoner. "Now tell us, what manner of creatures are your friends in shining armor who vexed us?"

"Paladins of Tyr."

"Tyr!" shrieked both fiends as though they'd been slapped.

"A greater power of Mount Celestia!" squealed Rejik.

"They seek this gate as well," offered Noph. "They'll be here soon, too. Perhaps we can all work together."

The vrocks looked down at Noph, then up at each other, and burst into fits of laughter. Around them, the manes chittered and slapped at each other playfully, and the bar-lgura shifted to the walls of the chamber. Using their chameleonlike ability, they blended with their surroundings.

"Here's the plan," thought Shaakat to Rejik. "We'll lay down a warding circle against creatures of law and goodness. You maintain it while the troops attack and I cast deadly magic until they're all dead!"

"Agreed, agreed! They can't survive that!"

In hedonistic anticipation of slaughter, they bent their wills upon the lesser tanar'ri once more and began to organize them for the ambush.

Chapter 6

Even if you want the job done right, have someone else do it. That way, you'll never get the blame.

"Khelben was right when he said there was a great force of evil at work here," whispered Miltiades.

The group lurked down the hall from the gate chamber, listening to the riot of fiends within. Miltiades handed Khelben's map to Aleena, who tucked it into a pocket. "The gate to the Utter East is just ahead, and it sounds as if the fiends are massing there. They must be involved in the kidnapping plot. They've probably been stationed there to intercept us!"

"So much the better," hissed Kern, hefting his hammer and gazing toward the noise with a glint in his eye. "Save a princess *and* destroy fiends! Tyr blesses us this day!"

"For the last time, *she's not a princess!*" moaned Aleena, rolling her eyes and shaking her head in exasperation.

"Whatever."

"We can't simply rush in there and start swinging," protested Trandon. "We have no idea of how many fiends we're up against."

Kern frowned at the warrior. "We know they stand between us and our quest, and we know the longer we wait, the more of them there will be to destroy. What more does a champion of Tyr need to know?"

"Nothing," agreed Jacob.

"All right," said Miltiades, ending the discussion with the tone of his voice. "The enemy is before us and our course is clear. Prepare for battle."

"Wait!" Aleena cried in a hushed voice. "Trandon's got a point. That sounds like an *army* of fiends in there."

Kern and Jacob groaned impatiently. Miltiades looked at her with an expression that reminded her that he used to be undead.

"Stop!" she hissed. "Look here. I've got a spell that'll let me look in that room and see what we're up against."

"I don't *want* to know the odds," whispered Kern.

"But intelligence can help us win the battle, or at least win it more quickly, with less casualties! That helps secure our mission. Remember? To save the *princess?*" She spat the last word with scorn.

"Shh!" cautioned Miltiades. "We waste time. Aleena cast your spell quickly and conduct your espionage. The rest of you prepare for the charge."

"And," added Kern, "she's not a princess."

Aleena took a deep breath to quell her rising irritation. As she released the air from her lungs, she reached into a narrow pocket at her hip and withdrew a bit of bat fur, which she ripped in half and placed into each palm. She rolled back her eyes and shut them, clenched her fists and touched the knuckles of her thumbs together, then pressed them against her full lips. She bowed her head and whispered into her closed hands. They began to glow red from the inside, as though each held a brilliantly illuminated pearl.

Without opening her eyes, Aleena looked down the corridor, toward the gate chamber. She briefly glanced down at her companions, who gazed at her face intently, unaware that she now looked upon them from above, with an invisible magical eye. Her sight turned back toward the rough, slightly curving corridor ahead and moved that way.

Aleena's eye paused at the entrance of the room, as she mentally gasped. The area would be dark but for the kaleidoscopic glow of the gate itself, at the far end of the chamber, which threw eerie light upon a room filled to the corners with fiends. She looked over a stormy sea of mindless, murderous manes. They crowded within the confines of the chamber, pushing, shoving and biting. Curiously, the manes refused to spill into the corridor, though no door or gate stood between them and her party. Obviously, some greater fiend kept them from stampeding into every available space.

Aleena turned her attention toward the gate and spied dark figures atop the pyramid, beside glowing tusks. A pair of tall silhouettes stood over a third creature, who lay at their feet. Slowly, she drifted closer, over the heads of the turbulent manes, penetrating the gloom, focusing upon the creatures by the gate. Her magical eye drifted higher and closer to them. At last she could make out the oily feathers, the scaly heads, the cruel beaks.

"Vrocks!" her lips pronounced, back in the corridor. "True tanar'ri! Some of the most powerful of fiends!"

"You flatter us, human scum-wizard," boomed Rejik's voice in her head, and both of the vulturelike fiends looked directly at her magical eye! "Except you should've said, *'The* most powerful of fiends!'"

"Tell the worms of Tyr to come out of hiding and face us, if they dare!" cried Shaakat. Across the room, the manes began to chatter and churn with escalating blood lust.

As Aleena looked past the vrocks, at the third figure on the floor of the pyramid's flat top, one of the vrocks extended its pair of shriveled humanoid arms and gestured toward her invisible eye. Her enchantment shattered and dissolved with a shimmering rain of sparks. Back in the corridor, she unclasped her fists and slapped her hands over eyes, throwing back her head in pain. Miltiades caught her as she reeled. She drew her hands from her eyes and blinked until she could see normally again.

"They know we're here," she said. "There's a mass of manes just a few feet away, and two vrocks atop the pyramid, next to the gate."

"Then it's time for justice!" cried Jacob.

"Battle positions!" ordered Kern.

"Hold," countered Miltiades. He squinted down the hallway, toward the enemy, so close yet not coming any closer. "They're waiting for us, aren't they?"

"Yes," said Aleena. "And there's more."

The men turned and looked at her expectantly.

"Kastonoph's in there! They've got him tied up at the top of the pyramid, by the gate."

The men gasped. "I thought you said Noph was dead," said Miltiades, looking at Trandon.

"They're probably creating an illusion of him to fool us," suggested Jacob.

"Maybe I was wrong," sputtered Trandon. "Maybe

they teleported him here to use against us." Miltiades stared hard at him. "Fiends teleport, don't they?"

"If Noph's in there, then there's no time to waste!" said Kern.

"Kern, if we launch a frontal assault, Noph won't live long," cautioned Aleena.

"If we don't destroy them immediately, Noph will die much too slowly," replied Miltiades evenly, turning to her. "But there's a trap awaiting us in there. I know fiends, and I know how they think. If they're just waiting for us when their hordes are only thirty feet away, with nothing *physical* to keep them from charging us, then it's obvious that they want us to enter and fight them there."

"What other choice do we have, Miltiades?" asked Kern. "The way is clear!"

"What about Noph?" asked Trandon.

"What about the ambush?" asked Aleena.

"Noph *is* their ambush," submitted Jacob. "They think we're vulnerable if they have a hostage, but Noph knew the risks when he came along. The quest is the only important thing."

Kern looked to Miltiades. "What'll we do?"

The elder paladin looked toward the gate chamber, teeming with fiends, then back toward the corridors from which they'd come. "One way or another, we've got to enter that chamber and take on those fiends. I think the only way to overcome the ambush, given the circumstances, is to charge straight through it."

"*Yes!*" cried Jacob. Kern moved to take the lead.

Miltiades reached out and caught his fellow paladin's muscular arm. "Not so fast. . . ."

* * * * *

"Where are they?" whined Rejik. "I never met a Tyrleech who could resist a challenge!"

"They're smart," answered Shaakat. "They're trying to come up with a plan to save our little human slave, here, but they'll soon realize the only option they have is to come in swinging. Just be ready with the warding circle."

Shaakat extended his wrinkled hands and whispered in his mind, "I call on *ggatzshriiegk*." Instantly, a shining obsidian javelin, covered from tip to tail with jagged scales, pierced the planar boundaries of the Abyss and flew to him, sizzling through the astral flow to the Prime Material, faster than time. With a black flash it appeared in his outstretched hands.

"The wizard is my first target," he thought, hefting the weapon for a throw. "The others will have to fight their way to us." The vrock mentally touched upon each of the bar-lgura, commanding them to wait upon his orders, while Rejik restrained the manes.

Another few minutes passed without the heroes' attack, and the fiendish troops again grew restless.

"Where *are* they?" repeated Rejik. "Why don't we just release the manes? Why don't we—"

At that moment, the resolute cry of human voices filled the cavern and three manes standing at the entrance squealed in agony, spinning violently from their feet as though struck by unseen fists. They tumbled limply to the ground with a spray of ichor and dissipated into thick black vapor. The fiends around them wailed in terror and began to crawl over each other in retreat. Four more screamed and split open with a vicious crush of invisible blows—they oozed upon the floor and began to smoke as well. Behind the advancing, invisible wall of slashing death, a bright flash briefly illuminated the shadowy profile of a humanoid before streaking like a comet to the center of the room and exploding in a massive ball of fire. The manes within the infernal blast shrieked horribly and collapsed into smoking puddles. Pandemonium erupted across the chamber. Acidic gases hung in the air where perhaps half or more of the manes had stood.

Shaakat cackled. "Excellent command of invisibility, to maintain it in battle."

Another tangle of sparks at the entrance to the room betrayed the transparent figure of the wizard, but this time the light was blue, and it crackled momentarily between the human's hands before shooting across the chamber in a jagged bolt of lightning. The vrocks tensed against the sting of magic and then thrust it off. The lightning passed through them and smote the wall behind with a thunderous eruption that shook the room. Their feathers stood up in the charged atmosphere around them, yet they took no hurt from the attack.

"Potent electrical assault. I almost felt it," sneered Shaakat. "Rejik, set the manes free and erect the ward. I'll take care of the rest."

Rejik released his mental hold upon the lesser fiends and focused his mind upon a line of blood, smeared along the perimeter of the pyramid's platform. He spread his wings and arms outward and froze in that position, bending his will upon making and holding a barrier as powerful as the one he and Shaakat had encountered in the Utter East. *This* one, however, would prove deadly to creatures of goodness and order.

Throughout the chamber, the unbridled manes clamored wildly and turned upon the invisible menace, swarming toward it. Bellows of hatred blended with howls of pain as the monsters crashed upon the circle of Tyr warriors and splattered backward. The heroes' transparent weapons shimmered in deadly arcs through the air as they slew the clawing fiends all around them. The manes piled upon one another. The chamber grew thick with the haze of their smoking dead remains.

"Time to show yourselves, cowardly primes," thought

Shaakat. He reached out with his keen senses, found the magical aura surrounding the Tyr followers, and obliterated it with a stroke of his powerful mind. With a sizzling hiss, the four human men and one woman shimmered into view. The warrior males formed a crescent of swinging weapons, mowing down the squealing manes before them, while the female wizard gestured, calling up another spell.

Quickly, the vrock drew back his spindly arm and hurled his javelin with the strength of a giant. It buzzed like a furious wasp as it sliced through the air, and its scales stood up from its surface, making it spin like a streaking top as it homed in on its target. The spear's gleaming point drove into the throng, passing through two manes uninhibited, and bore into the chest of the wizard, knocking her from her feet with a cry of astonishment. "I call on *ggatzshriiegk*," thought Shaakat and the weapon twirled cruelly in the wizard's body, eliciting a delicious scream of agony from her, before ripping free and sailing back to him.

To Shaakat's delight, a mob of tanar'ri swarmed over the woman as quickly as she fell to the ground! Her arms and legs flailed beneath the sweeping host of scratching, gnawing manes, but she couldn't find her feet. One of the warriors turned and desperately slung his warhammer at the piling fiends, reaching into their midst with his free hand to seize hers, then snatching it back as they snapped greedily at him. He cried out "Aleena!" as he fought through the horde, and a second warrior turned to help, but it was too late.

Both vrocks cackled joyfully in the echo of the warriors' cries of anguish.

"*Nooo!*" wailed Noph from the ground behind them, his magical charm broken at the sight. "Aleena! You *bastards!*" he cursed and began to sob. The master fiends laughed harder.

"You wish to fight unseen?" asked Shaakat in the Tyr-lovers' minds as he sent forth utter darkness from his own mind, plunging the entire party of humans into blindness. At the same time, he cocked his arm to hurl his javelin at another one of them. Then he paused.

Amazing! The humans were fighting completely blind and slaughtering the manes while suffering little damage themselves! They shouted to each other and moved into a defensive circle, allowing themselves plenty of room to swing, then entered into a warrior's dance, thrashing the space around them in a graceful series of attacks that crushed and scattered the tanar'ri. One of them—a warrior completely sheathed in shining plates of finely wrought metal—spun about, holding his gleaming hammer at arm's length while he twirled and uttered sickening words of goodness and light—and the darkness fell.

"I want to attack, too!" complained Rejik in his head.

"Just keep that warding circle intact, leatherhead! They're still coming this way!"

Shaakat flung his deadly javelin again, aiming for the one who banished his arcane darkness, but the human anticipated his throw and swung his hammer to meet it. The flat of the paladin's mallet squarely met the point of the spear with a resounding *crack*, and the fiend's prized weapon splintered into black rubble that flew back to the pyramid and rattled against its surface like a hail storm.

The paladin with hair the color of fire and armor like the scales of a golden fish held up his hammer and cried, *"In Tyr's name, be gone!"* His voice echoed through the chamber like a titan's, and all around the warriors a dozen manes convulsed and ruptured into black smoke. The stinging residue of slaughtered manes grew dense, and the fighters choked and reeled. Shaakat leaped upon the opportunity.

"Now," thought the vrock to the bar-lgura, who rippled forth from the walls of the chamber and sprang at the paladins with fore- and hindclaws extended. The humans parried their savage slashing and biting attacks, yet the one wielding a staff rolled to the ground under the crush of a leaping bar-lgura. The tanar'ri seized the fighter by the throat and released its Abyssal aura of terror; the prime gagged with sudden fear. He dropped his weapon and struggled frantically to get free of the fiend, which leaned over to clamp its vicelike jaws upon his face. The remaining manes in the room converged upon the fallen man, climbing atop one another to get at him.

"Trandon's down!" shouted the warrior with a large blade, and the remaining three humans shifted smoothly to a triangle defense. Onward they pressed. The remaining manes burst into roiling puffs of toxic vapor, and their spirits fled back to the Abyss. The bar-lgura leapt in groups, hoping to overwhelm the paladins, only to be driven back on their heels until, one by one, they too fled for their native plane.

At last, bloody and weaving from their battles, the three warriors of Tyr reached the base of the pyramid and began to climb its steps. Side by side they ascended, grim-faced, readying their weapons for another bout. The two vrocks waited at the top.

"Paladins beware!" shouted Noph.

Shaakat wheeled and slapped the young man with the back of his emaciated hand. Noph cried out and lay still.

"Yes, beware paladins of Tyr," sneered Shaakat in their heads, returning his gaze to them. "We have your impudent whelp here. Surrender or we'll murder him right now!"

"Let them kill me!" mumbled Noph through bleeding, fattened lips.

"You shall be remembered with honor, Freeman Kastonoph!" cried the red-headed human.

The paladins continued their ascent without hesitation. Shaakat hissed and raised his arms as if to strike at them, but waited for them to reach the top.

As one, they stepped up to the top of the pyramid, sword and hammers raised high, but as their feet touched the warding line of blood, a bright flash erupted in front of each of them with a shrill *crack*, casting them back down the steps like rag dolls. They tumbled downward with a clatter of metal and groans of misery, coming to rest in a heap at the pyramid's base. Shaakat and Rejik roared with laughter.

"Kern!" cried one. "Kern, rise in the name of Tyr!" The paladin in golden scales shook his head and weakly rolled to his knees.

"Jacob?" called the elder warrior to the swordsman, who lay still and lifeless. "Jacob!" The human looked up at the vrocks with an expression of hatred to warm a tanar'ri's heart. "Damned fiends! Tyr, grant me the power to fight once more!"

The two paladins pulled themselves to their feet and began to climb once more. "This is it, Miltiades," said the one called Kern. "It's now or never!"

"That's it! Come a little closer," thought Rejik to them. He broke his concentration upon the ward and stepped closer to his partner, at the top of the steps, watching the humans stumble toward them. "Creatures of law," he sneered. "They never quit. It's their greatest weakness!"

The paladins fully regained their feet about halfway up the stairs and began to gain speed. Their hammers swooped down and around, then curved upward on their backswings, coming over the top with deadly force as the warriors gained the last few steps. They opened their mouths and bellowed with holy righteousness. The fiends spread their wings in response and spewed forth a swath of stringy, greenish fluid; then they blinked themselves to the side. The paladins' weapons caught only air, while they themselves were drenched in the tanar'ri's deadly, viscous juices.

The spores hatched with lightning speed, nourished by the wholesome flesh of the Tyr worshipers; vines wrapped them tightly, thrusting into their bodies.

The two men rolled down the steps and came to rest atop the third, who gave no protest as he received their full weight. The elder paladin twitched in his death throes for a few moments before the last glimmer of his life faded away.

Noph's stomach turned as he watched the vrocks caper in an obscene victory dance. They cawed in horrifying, otherworldly laughter as they circled each other. His eyes filled and spilled over, blurring the ghastly vision. Angrily he blinked away the tears and cast his gaze about the room, seeking the specter of death coming to claim his unworthy life.

His eyes went wide, then he looked up at his tormentors.

"You sickening pair of Abyssal garbage trolls!" he snarled at them. "I've seen some spineless, yellow-bellied, scum-sucking cowards in Faerûn, but I never knew it got that much worse in the Abyss!"

The vrocks stumbled to a standstill in the midst of their dance and stared down at the helpless human.

"You think you're so tough; just untie me and give me one of those hammers! One-on-one or both of you together, I'll kick you from here to Elminster's tower and back!"

"The little berk wants us to untie him. How *sweet!*" jeered Rejik. "Let's do it."

"Bah! There's no sport in squashing bugs," scoffed Shaakat.

"I'll squash your ugly pointy heads, birdbrain! If you've got guts, I'll spread 'em all over this room!"

"How about a hunt?" suggested Rejik. "Give him thirty seconds to run."

"Wait!" cried Shaakat. He hopped closer to Noph and glared into his eyes. "He's not thinking of fighting *or* running." The vrock leaned into the boy's face, making him wince and shut his eyes tight. "He's thinking . . . *distraction!*"

The vrocks spun about with a rush of feathers. Miltiades, Kern, Jacob, Trandon, and Aleena were standing inside the warding circle. They were completely unharmed and grinning ever so slightly.

In unison, Shaakat and Rejik emitted a paralyzing screech. The humans cringed in pain and leaped to the defensive, and the vrocks took advantage of the moment. They disappeared with a *pop* and fled for the Abyss with all the speed they could muster.

"Victory!" shouted Aleena.

"Justice!" cheered the followers of Tyr.

"You used the magical mirror, didn't you?" said Noph.

"Smart boy!" answered Kern, kneeling down to release him. "Well done, Freeman Kastonoph!" said the younger paladin, imitating Miltiades' rolling burr and tone of voice.

"Well done, indeed," echoed the elder paladin, himself, taking no note of the jest. "You risked your life to draw the fiends' attention so we could cross the warding line without delay. That took a paladin's courage and wisdom."

"It would've been worth it," said Noph while Kern and Aleena massaged the feeling back into his extremities. "For the quest," he declared, looking at Aleena. She smiled softly and ruffled his hair. Noph sighed in contentment.

"You were in little danger, actually," said Trandon. "Seeing what our reflections went through allowed us to prepare for a lightning strike of our own. Those tanar'ri would've been bad-smelling gas before they could lay a claw on you."

"That's right," agreed Kern, and his face grew serious. "We couldn't lose you."

Noph stared up at the youthful paladin. "C-couldn't lose me?" he asked, perplexed. "But—I've been the fifth wheel, the 'chaos child,' the 'foolish youngling.'"

"You accepted the quest, in spite of your weaknesses," replied Miltiades. "You are a member of the rescue team." He patted Noph's head. "You are one of us."

The ancient knight looked at the group around him and pointed toward the enchanted arch of mammoth tusks. "There lies the next stage of our quest. Thanks to our noble reflections, who died for us, we are fresh and ready to continue. If Freeman Kastonoph is ready, let us activate the gate and proceed!"

"Gentlemen, there's a *damsel* in need of rescuing out there," cried Kern with a wink at Aleena. "May Tyr guide us!"

"Tyr!" shouted the other warriors. Noph merely stared at the portal and gulped.

"*Open in the name of the past and present lords of Waterdeep!*" called Miltiades in his deep, rolling voice. The flowing veins of magic within the tusks dimmed and disappeared while a thin ripple of yellow light spread across the plane of the portal. The wall of the gate chamber no longer appeared beyond the archway; within, all was darkness.

One by one they cautiously stepped through, weapons drawn and readied—first Miltiades, then Kern, Jacob, and Trandon. Noph stood at the threshold, squinting into the void. He turned and looked back at Aleena.

"I don't know if I should go on," he said in a small voice. "I'm tired. I'm so, so *tired*—and I'm scared, Aleena. I don't think I'm cut out to be a hero anymore."

The wizardess put her hand on his shoulder and squeezed warmly. "I don't blame you, but they need you."

"*They* need *me?*"

"I'm not going on, Noph."

Noph stared at the beautiful enchantress, open-mouthed. "But why?"

"I have several reasons, but I can't explain them here and now. The important thing is you're the only Waterd-havian left in the party. *You're* Khelben's eyes and ears, now. You're my father's sole remaining champion." She looked deeply into his eyes. "Please, Kastonoph. I won't force you to go, but I will beg."

"No! Don't beg! I can't stand putting you in that position. I'll go."

"Thank you, Noph. Thank you from me, from the Nine Lords of Waterdeep, from all of the Western Heartlands!"

Kastonoph turned back to the portal, pulled his knife from its boot sheath, and took a deep breath. "I had no *idea* how quickly the gods give you what you ask for," he mumbled as he stepped through and disappeared into the Utter East.

"Close in the name of the past and present lords of Waterdeep," Aleena bade the gate. She moved to the corridor leading out of the chamber. Then, summoning her most potent magic, she hurled a lightning bolt at the gate and the roof of the chamber over it. The ceiling buckled and collapsed, and tons of stone thundered down into the corridor, throwing up a haze of dust and rubble. Aleena looked critically at her work for a moment. Then she murmured, "Well, that's done," and turned back the way the party had come.

Somewhere in Undermountain, Halaster laughed.

Epilogue

Kill the messenger; it doesn't solve the problem, but you've got to admit it feels right.

    The Abyss never looked so good.
    Shaakat and Rejik reveled in the sound of the death-wind, blowing through the void. Rejik ripped huge chunks of flint from the cavern floor, for sheer joy.
    "Paladins," Shaakat sneered angrily.
    "Never again," returned Rejik.

"Report," commanded General Raachaak, appearing out of nowhere and ringing their brains with the ferocity of his thoughts. They shrieked in surprise and trembled before the gigantic, winged tanar'ri.

"We discovered a gate within the city of the bloodforge, and learned its other side lay in another part of the world, called Undermountain," thought Shaakat hastily.

"A slice of the Abyss, it was," added Rejik. "A wondrous place!"

"I know of it, and Skullport as well. Continue."

"We found the gate in Undermountain, but it was defended by paladins of Tyr!"

"Tyr! A greater power of Mount Celestia! Perhaps the upper planars are planning to acquire the bloodforge!" The general gritted his fangs in consternation. "Did you destroy the paladins?"

"Yes, indeed!" cried Shaakat. "But they destroyed the gate before they died!"

The balor reared his head and bellowed in rage, filling the vast emptiness with his terrifying cry. "Miserable failures!" he snarled, gazing upon the vrocks.

"Not failures! Not failures!" insisted Shaakat. "You ordered us to discover a way into the city of the bloodforge, and we did! We can find another way in!"

"The gate was a bad way in anyhow!" cried Rejik. "The side in the city of the bloodforge was surrounded by many, many powerful fighters!"

"I *will* find a way into that city!" declared Raachaak, freeing his whip, "but *you* will not!"

The sixty-fifth level of the Abyss is an empty, infinite place, but at that moment it was filled to its borders with the sound of cracking leather and piteous screaming.

WELCOME TO THE UTTER EAST!

THE DOUBLE DIAMOND TRIANGLE SAGA

The story continues . . .

The bride of the Open Lord of Waterdeep has been abducted. The kidnappers are from the far-off lands of the Utter East. But who are they? And what do they really want? Now a group of brave paladins must travel to the perilous kingdoms of this unknown land to find the answers. But in this mysterious world, nothing is ever quite what it appears.

Look for the forthcoming books in the series

Coming in January

THE MERCENARIES
By Ed Greenwood

In the mysterious land of the Utter East, a shadowy figure hires a group of unemployed pirates to aid him in a dangerous mission. What is their connection to the kidnapping of a young bride that has taken place in the faraway city of Waterdeep? Behind the mission lies a hidden purpose. Yet secrets may be revealed as you follow the quest of the mercenaries.

Coming in February

ERRAND OF MERCY
By Roger E. Moore

The paladins sent by the Lord of Waterdeep to rescue his kidnapped bride have arrived in a kingdom of the Utter East. The monarch seems friendly; but the kingdom is beset by menacing fiends. Before the ruler agrees to help the paladins in their quest, there is just one small task they must perform . . . .

Coming in March

AN OPPORTUNITY FOR PROFIT
By Dave Gross

The pirates hired to assassinate the kidnapped Waterdeep bride are hot on the trail. Having landed on the shores of the Utter East, they face fiendish perils and desperate dangers—all without knowing the identity of their employer. Now fate has set them on a collision course with others whose motives are quite different from their own.